Beast & Thorn

A REALM OF REVELRY FAERIETALES

CHELSEY ANN TOMPKINS

Written by

CHELSEY ANN TOMPKINS

A Realm of Revelry Series
Curse & Spindle
Straw & Gold
Beast & Thorn

A Conduit of Light Trilogy
A Conduit of Light
A Baron of Bonds
A Blightress of Wrath

for all the ones who sang
"Belle's Reprise"
with their whole fucking chest

Pronunciation Guide

Characters

Reshina, REH-SHE-NUH
Arthur, ARE-THUR
Piffle, PIFF-ULL
Ishtak, ISH-TALK
Seraphine, SARA-FEEN
Korven, CORE-VEN
Morella, MORE-EL-UH
Killian, KILL-E-EN

Places

Riche REE-SH

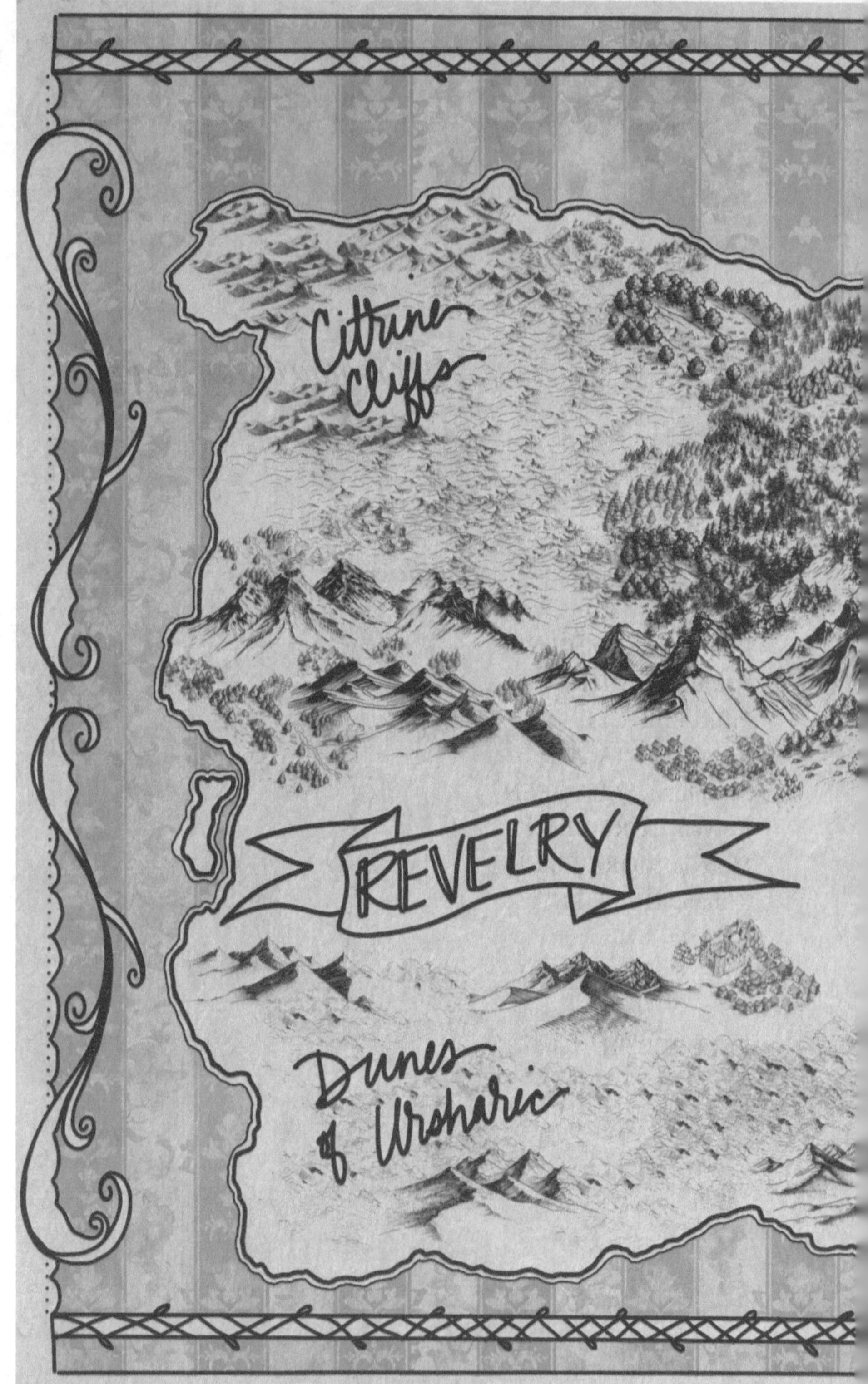

Citrine Cliffs
REVELRY
Dunes of Ursharic

Silver Isle
Moonstone Wood
Brakish Wood
Heartstone Wood
Havenshire
Riche
Songbird Cove
CAT

CHAPTER 1

Arthur

THE INEVITABILITY THAT I WOULD BECOME A CURSED man for the rest of my days came by letter on a mild spring evening. The roses bloomed with sickening vitality, the crimson petals brightening each hall of my castle.

I stood before the fireplace in my mother's room, staring at the quick scrawl across the soft parchment, skimming it first for any hope that this last chance to escape my curse would end in good fortune.

Dear Arthur, King of Heartstone,

This letter is to inform you that Killian, King of the Citrine Cliffs, cannot help your mother. The king is saddened to hear of the untimely death of your friend Prince Urik and his betrothed. However, I must bestow the unfortunate news that though the king received Prince Urik's letter requesting help to change your mother from human into faekind, he is not in the authority to do so.

Handing out favors to humans and all that. The

Goddesses simply wouldn't hear of it. And Killian is in enough trouble as it is, but I digress.

Best of luck in your endeavors,

Fedir Westwind,
First Captain to the King of the Citrine Cliffs

Post Script,
My condolences for your mother's declining health, of course.

I CRUMPLED THE LETTER IN MY FIST, BREAKING THE golden wax seal into pieces before tossing it into the fire. The flames licked the parchment clean to ash, an immaculate representation of my future.

Staring at the hearth, I didn't know which sound to focus on first—the knocking at the door or the rasping lungs of my mother lying prone in her bed. The door won out in the end, and as I bid the little man to enter, he did so loudly, scuffling to my mother with some new tincture.

"There you are, M'lady," Piffle cooed, tipping a mug of something repugnant to her lips. "This will keep those nasty raspies out." My mother wheezed again, but sipped as she was told.

The short, shuffling footsteps of our family's singular servant headed my way. "Was the letter to your liking, Master Arthur?"

I bit down on the words I would have liked to say. And say them I might have in another room. In another time, when my mother was not succumbing to rasping sickness and leaving the Curse of Heartstone Castle to her only child.

"No, Piff," I answered finally. "It was not."

"You've more time, sir," he whispered, not daring to raise his voice enough for my mother to hear. "She had a good night. And there are others in Revelry with great powers. Perhaps the Goddess of the—"

I sank further into the fireside chair, spilling my long legs out in front of me, interrupting his unrealistic words of hope. "No, Piff. Time is the one thing that might save me." I leaned my head back against the rest, closing my eyes to the sound of my mother hacking up whatever Piffle had given her. "And time is the one thing I have squandered. The one thing I have not."

The squat little man had the decency to bow his head. The golden tips of his pointed ears shone brilliant in the firelight, enhanced by the many golden rings pierced through each one. "Tell me, sire. What can I do?"

I clasped my hands, settling in to rest my mind and prepare myself for what the morning might bring. "Fall into the Underrealm, Piff. Find me there and plunge a dagger into my heart."

CHAPTER 2

Reshina

"And just how many cattle do you own, Mister Brough?" I tilted my head back with the question, draining the last of the yagsmead before tossing the small glass back to the barkeep. "Another," I ordered, dragging the delicate lace of my sleeve across my mouth.

"Near seventy-five, love. Over ninety after the calves come realmside this s-spring." The man's slur was creeping in, loosening his tongue. I gave him another quick glance over. Grey streaks licked his temples, giving him that distinguished gentlemanly look. He was handsome in a sort of rugged way and laying it on thick since I'd sat down next to him at the bar. It was obvious he had no idea he was speaking to a Goddess, and even more clear he presumed our conversation would lead to a quick fuck in the alleyway if he charmed me enough.

I raised a brow at his numbers, knocking back another glass, barely pausing between my next barrage of questions. "Where would such a stout herder find the land to keep so many cows? We are not far from Heartstone Castle, true? Is your king so generous with such a large partaking of land?" I set my elbow on the worn bar top, landing my chin onto my fist. "I can only imagine your taxes, Mister Brough."

A secretive grin pulled at his mouth and he crooked a finger, urging me closer. I bit my tongue, leaning in to hear his answer. "The King of Heartstone Castle has not been seen in over a decade, my sweet. And he ain't been collecting no taxes, neither." The simple herder grabbed his mug of ale, tipping it towards me. "Fine by me, I say. I use up the land the way that's best. Don't need no high-born to tell me where I can and can't feed me herd." He smacked an open palm against the counter, raising his voice and his finger. "I was born and raised in Heartstone and if anyone deserves more land than he was born with, it'd be me, not some scarred up boy, pretendin' to rule—"

"Boy?" I interrupted. "I heard King Arthur is well past forty."

He waved a hand dismissively, slopping the contents of his mug on the bar. "Summat like that. Don't know, really." He took a long drink. "When I came to this town, he was off in Riche, spendin' his coin on all sorts of unkingly things. Like gamblin'. And women."

He winked over his mug, and I narrowed my eyes ever so slightly. "Didn't you just mention you were born and raised here?"

"Oh, I uhh..."

"And if you were not, which I assume is the actual truth, doesn't that mean that you have very little claim on any of the land in Heartstone Wood, Mister Brough?" I paused for emphasis, allowing the truth of my ruse to settle in. "And assuming you have not stolen half your herd from farmers of the Brackish Wood, which I suspect you have, do you not have even *less* claim on the land of the Ravenfae? Where you have taken your herd without the permission of the Ravenfae Goddess Reshina?"

The time for pleading and begging at my knees was then, but the idiot had not yet caught on to just who he was talking to. "I-I don't know what y-you're talking ab—"

I dropped my cloak, revealing my black feathered wings tipped in silver. He gasped in awe, likely never having seen a

Goddess before. I grabbed the collar of his jacket in one quick swipe, smiling in true humor, watching the man peel himself off his barstool and begin begging with cries of mercy.

It turned out to be quite the spectacle in the single tavern of Heartstone—whimsically named *The Withering Rose.* For in sudden shock and fear, the man understood he was speaking to *me*, Reshina, Goddess of the Veil and Goddess of the Ravenfae—former Cursebringer of Revelry and current protector of my people.

"Let this be a lesson to you, Mister Brough," I began, allowing my voice to rise, in the sudden silence. "Let this be a lesson for all of you. The Brackish Wood is not unoccupied, nor is it ruler-less like this desolate place you call a kingdom." I threw him across the room where he crashed into a table, knocking it and its occupants to the ground. "Now," I said with a mocking grin. "As you all know, even a Goddess of the Veil cannot burn this tavern down to the ground without dire consequences." I pulled up the hem of my black silken skirts, kicking a chair out of my way as I took my time walking toward the thief I'd been seeking for the better part of a week.

"You can thank your ancestors for that treaty between the fae and human kingdoms. You are lucky, my friends, that it is I whom you have scorned with your thievery and not another Goddess of the Veil who would take a more...destructive interest in your little tavern, treaty or no." I stood in front of the man as he cowered on the floor, attempting to shield his face from my sight. I dug into my pocket, searching by feel alone for the correct glass vial. "Alas, I have no love for the scent of burning flesh, but I do have a penchant for delivering a curse to a soul in need of repentance."

"No!" he shouted, shaking below me. "Please! Have mercy!"

"Mercy?" I laughed from deep within my chest. "Mercy comes from the hands of the Goddessblessed, not the Goddess-cursed." I uncorked the vial, spilling the deep emerald smoke and sand over his boots. "Come now," I soothed as he began to sob. "Join me, Mister Brough, in the timeless dance of living a cursed life."

CHAPTER 3

The Beast

GET BACK UNDERGROUND, YOU MONGREL. YOU'LL GIVE US *frostbite. Your time is almost up anyway.*

HUNGER.

Still? Get on with the hunt, then.

SMELL CREATURE.

Goddess save me.

NOT DEER.

A cow again? Much preferable than the rotten sheep you found last week. I couldn't move the rest of the day, and—

WOMAN.

...Stop.

HUNGER.

Turn around.

HUNGER.

Get underground now!

HUNGER FOR WOMAN.

Goddess fucking dammit. BEAST. HEAR THIS. TURN AROUND NOW AND I WILL GRANT YOU ANOTHER FULL DAY AND NIGHT ABOVE.

LET ME OUT?

YES. ONLY IF YOU GET BELOW RIGHT NOW.

WOMAN CLOSE.

Is she really worth losing two days above?

YES.

You've done this to yourself, then.

YOU LIE.

I have not. I've warned you before that this would happen.

NO...CONTROL...ME...HUNGER.

You cannot have her. Let me take the reins.

I STAY.

Stop resisting. You'll bruise my ribs again.

CLAW. STAY. HUNGER. WOMAN.

I'm sorry, but I must do this. She is not yours to take.

NEED.

You think you do, but we've gotten along just fine without.

YOU NEED.

Ha. Now you're concerned for me, eh? She must be something.

GET FOR YOU.

Stop resisting me. Get your hairy ass underground.

BRINGER.

Bringer? What is that?

BRINGER FROM VEIL.

Bringer from... Leave! Leave right now!

BLOOD.

What?

BLOOD SPILLED. SMELL.

You couldn't have. I would know if you—

BRINGER BLEED.

On this land?

BRINGER COMING TO YOU.

Now?

NOW.

Fuck.

CHAPTER 4

Reshina

Granting Mister Brough the courtesy of explaining how to break his curse was considerably kind of me, and certainly not necessary. The title of Cursebringer was no longer mine, but my son's current burden to bear, and I was no longer held to the rules of the job. I had handed that position to Korven over a decade ago, though old habits of delivering curses still got the better of me.

After I'd dragged the thief out of *The Withering Rose* and past the boundary of the nearby Heartstone Castle, I explained how he might find a way out of the harrowing future before him. He was now bound to his boots, cursed to walk over every inch of Revelry until one of two things occurred. He could walk over every rock, speck of sand, and snowy mountainside in all of Revelry without rest or he could find another soul to carry him back to the tavern without his boots ever touching the ground.

It was a particularly nasty curse to break and had come from the Veil three decades ago, meant for a young woman of barely twenty. Alas, as fate would have it, she perished before I could deliver it to her on the night of the Cursed Moon, and thus, I had kept it with me ever since.

It was rare that a curse was not delivered, but I'd seen it

enough in my previous hundreds of years as Cursebringer to expect it every now and again. If the person the curse was meant for died before it could be delivered, I could easily bottle it, packing it away in a small glass vial until I saw fit to deliver to another at my whim.

Mister Brough's speck crossed the horizon as I perched on a bare branch of a tall, withered tree. In my raven form, I could see for miles as the brilliant silver moon shone over all the land of Heartstone, illuminating the world in crisp white over the snow.

Debating whether I should fly back to my own castle in the Brackish Wood or attempt to sleep inside the noticeably abandoned Heartstone Castle, I wondered what *had* happened to the current King of Heartstone?

When I had delivered a curse to his father, the current King Arthur had not yet existed in this world. The last time I'd seen the late king of Heartstone, he'd been no more than a raging Beast, ravaging his land, bound to his castle's boundary, searching always for the woman who could break his curse.

Whomever he did find had given him a child, but must not have given him the one thing he needed to break from the Beast; someone who loved him.

Whispers of a *new* Beast, far larger and monstrous than the last, had come to my ears in the Brackish Wood over the last decade. And so, as it sometimes was, the original curse had not been broken, but sent down the familial line onto his son, Arthur.

Pity.

The longer it took the curse to break, the stronger it would become.

Curiosity is a dangerously wicked thing; I've always cautioned my children of this. And as I descended from the hollow branch, shifting back into my Ravenfae form, I was careless to disregard my own advice.

Darkness fell upon me as I landed in the castle's shadow,

bringing something sinister to the winter air. The chill bit sharply, gnawing at my fingertips as I brushed away fresh snow atop a headstone, leaning in the frozen earth. Just below the staircase to the great castle doors, the marker had been placed at the very edge of the last stone—I imagined so a visitor could not enter without acknowledging the dead.

Marianna Dubois, Queen of Heartstone, Duchess of Riche

I dared not speak the name aloud, for I knew the Veil to be a fragile line next to the buried dead, or newly born, and I had no desire to invoke the spirit of the woman once bound to the curse of the land.

An overgrown bush of roses grew beside her grave. Its thick vines were adorned with sharp thorns, black as the gown I donned each day, and sharp as my daughter's foul mouth.

A smile lifted my lips thinking of Morella, imagining the wild minx of a girl King Killian of the Citrine Cliffs would soon be married to in an arrangement made thirteen years past.

I carelessly swept away more of the ice frozen to the grave, chipping at the date the Queen of Heartstone had died when my sleeve brushed across a particularly sharp thorn of the rosebush. Cursing under my breath, I pulled away sharply, snagging the fine lace and ripping open the skin along my palm. Three drops of fresh blood fell from my hand before I clutched it to my chest.

Now, I've always prided myself in my vast memory of the curses I've delivered. Each one has belonged to me as its caretaker before I delivered it to its host. Each curse has varied in strength—most easy enough to live with—some a thinly veiled tragedy to those unlucky enough to receive it.

But though I've always remembered the bearers of the curses themselves with distinction, the details of each curse have grown foggy over my centuries of deliverance.

If I had paused just a moment to recall the finer points of the curse over Heartstone Castle, I would have been far more careful not to bleed onto the land.

In a sudden panic, the elements of the curse flooded my mind, bringing forth what I'd said to the late king all those years before.

And you shall remain a Beast until your natural death unless a maiden bleeds upon your land, becoming captive to your whims. But be warned, if she should not love you in each of your forms, the curse will remain unbroken and you will live out the rest of your days with a woman who cannot save you, lest she drive a blade into your heart, setting herself free and sending you to your grave.

With the memory of my words long since spoken into the evening air, the ground below rumbled, shaking loose the black petals of the winter blooms over the gravestone.

No. No, this couldn't be.

I repeated the words over and over in my head even as the land split, and I fell through, tumbling over rock and dirt and stone. Like a maw of jagged teeth, I fell through the land as it scraped over my skin and cut at my gown, pulling my black feathers by their barbs.

No magic could save me, but I did not fall into the earth without a fight. My fingers clawed at the roots in my descent, my fingernails snagging in wet earth, breaking and tearing as I tried and failed to stop my fall. The pull was impossible to counter with the magic from the Veil setting its course over me. I felt the curse settle there, just as I'd felt my own curse centuries ago nestle into my skin.

The tumble took as much of the fight in me as it could, but I was stronger. For a split moment, I stopped, my hand grasping a jutting rock, my fingers scraped and bloody over the stone. I dangled there, waiting for what, I couldn't say, as I had no room to shift and no clear way back to the top. In the growing dark, my fingers began to slip just before a hand wrapped around my ankle, tugging at my flesh, and aiding my plummet into the looming doom that was the pinnacle of my fate.

The Ravenfae Goddess of the Veil, brought to her lowest point, tumbled into the darkness that consumed all light. When I fell, I landed with a sharp crack, my wrist catching on the floor of a tunnel paved in stone. I breathed with fury and disbelief, my lungs heaving through the pain of a shattered bone broken through the skin of my wrist. My whimper was slight, but all sound echoed endlessly through the dark tunnel, including the harsh whisper of my captor.

"*Reshina?*"

Goddessdamn me, how could I have been so foolish?

"Yes," I breathed, sitting up, cradling my broken wrist with my still bleeding hand.

"Ravenfae Goddess?" he whispered in clear disbelief.

I shook my head at my carelessness, even though I replied with a gritted, "*Yes.*"

The man fell on bended knees, yanking my hand forward, inspecting the cut across my palm. Before I could pull it back, he traced over the fresh blood, bringing his fingers to his lips. His tongue met the crimson stain and a low laugh tumbled from his chest, reverberating off the rough hewn walls lit in candlelight from the sconces lining the tunnel path.

I pulled my hand back to my chest, seething at his response. So here was the King of Heartstone. Here was the man whose curse I was now bound to. I lifted my chin through the pain. "I cannot fathom what could be so humorous, Your Majesty. Do you so often laugh at a woman broken and bleeding on your doorstep?"

His laughter halted in an abrupt rumble. He stood, sinking his hands into his pockets. "I find it humorous, Goddess, that it is *you* of all the souls of Revelry who should bleed on my land." Another laugh escaped him, both mad and humorless. "You brought this curse upon this kingdom. And..." He paused, cocking his head as he looked me over. "You are perhaps the single soul who could never break it."

He turned and walked away, leaving me to bleed on the stone beneath the earth. "Welcome to the Underrealm," he called over his shoulder, adding after a pause, "Cursed Goddess of the Veil."

CHAPTER 5

Arthur

BRINGER.

"Quiet."

BRINGER HERE.

"Yes," I spat through gritted teeth. "I know. Go to sleep."

TWO DAYS FREE.

I stopped abruptly on the steps leading out of the tunnel. "Absolutely not. You refused to leave when I offered that deal."

LEFT.

"Only after I forced my control over you. Now shut up and rest. I've got to think."

YOU NEED BRINGER.

The Beast's last words rang through my thoughts before I felt him drift, closing our connection.

"Sire!"

"What!" I spun in a rage, my grating tone echoing behind me.

Piff shrank, curling in on himself and lowering his head. I hadn't even noticed him appear in front of me. "Sorry to disturb you, Master, but the woman…she is bleeding, is she not?"

I glanced behind me as if I'd be able to see her. "Patch her up.

We don't need a frenzy on our hands. Goddess or no, they'd tear her apart if she got too close."

"Goddess!" Piff shrieked, shrinking again as I gave him a withering look.

I nodded, softening my tone. "Of the Ravenfae, yes. I expect you to take care of her needs while she is here. She needn't be wandering down any dark corridors, do you understand?"

His black eyes bulged deep in their sockets as his gnarled hands covered his mouth. When he lowered them, I saw the grin that remained. "She's the one," he attempted to whisper, failing in the most irritating way. "A Goddess could save you! She can break the curse!"

"She cannot," I said dismissively. "Not in the way you're thinking, Piff." I continued up the staircase, meeting the landing that led to the endless corridors of the Underrealm.

He followed, postponing my earlier command to stop her bleeding. "Oh, sire, do not be so hard on yourself! Any woman could love you and that Beast! All we need to do is—"

"She cannot!" My words echoed around us and I sighed heavily. "She cannot love me. Ever. Now go."

"But—"

"Go, Piff. Or I'll barricade you in the western corridor."

"Master," he clucked, "you need me too much for me to believe such empty threats."

"One day I will be dead. I will not need you then, old friend."

His strange laughter trickled behind me as he rushed down the stairs. "Even then, I shall need to dig your grave, sire!"

I chuckled, entering the marbled hall, muttering under my breath. "Sooner than you think."

WHEN I LIFTED MYSELF FROM THE FLOOR, A TRAIL OF blood followed, staining the dusty slab of stone below my feet. I'd heal quickly from the wound as soon as I could bind it and get through the excruciating pain of setting the bone back into my ragged skin.

I looked up to find that the hole I fell through had closed. The tunnel ceiling had righted itself with no evidence I had ever fallen through it.

Dragged, more like. The King of Heartstone had aided my rather unorthodox appearance into the realm below Revelry, and we had a score to settle already.

I'd never been to the Underrealm. Upon reflection, I couldn't recall any of the other eleven Goddesses saying they had either. Ishtak, Goddess of the Underrealm, ruled over the Underfae and wasn't exactly a welcoming soul.

But it was Ishtak whom I would need to find.

She lurked somewhere in this Goddessforsaken realm of dank stone and dirt. If anyone knew how to get me out of this curse, it would be her.

"Pardon me, Your Exaltedness."

I rarely startled but jumped at the golden sconce speaking

to me.

"My apologies!" it cried, donning two blinking eyes and a droll little mouth. "I have come to assist you with your wounds!"

I sighed heavily, cradling my wrist and assessing how best to slip the bone back into place. "I am not in need of assistance from a gibbering candlestick."

"Oh! But I am not always such a thing!"

I stepped back in surprise. A little man, reaching just to my elbow, appeared beside me in a flash of gold shimmer. He wore the finely detailed burgundy jacket of a servant, immaculately pressed. His hair was a curly brown with bits of white ashes tufted throughout that he quickly brushed aside. With a crinkled face and large eyes, it was easy to look past his pointed ears, ending in skin the color of molten gold.

"Ah, a Changlingfae," I concluded, focusing back to my painful task at hand.

"The Goddess knows all!" he squeaked, turning his large set eyes to my wrist.

"Nonsense," I muttered, "your golden ears have given you away. And the fact that you were no more than wall decor but a moment ago." I took a full deep breath, then another. "Is that your Changlingfae power, then? To shift into a light source?" At the last of my words I gripped my hand, snapping it over the jutting bone. I whimpered in muted cries, taking more breaths before I opened my eyes to assess my progress.

"Precious Goddess, no!" he shouted in a high pitch bellow. "My gift is healing! The wall was just a bit of an introduction. Now here, let me see—"

His gnarled hands reached for my own and I stepped back. "I don't need your help, Changelingfae." I thought for half a moment, adding, "Not for this anyway."

"But I—"

"I've been healing my own wounds longer than you've

existed in this realm, Revelry or otherwise. Now let me tend to my—"

"Pardon, Oh Greatest Goddess of the Realm, but I must insist on my assistance!"

The voice came from the golden bandage which appeared suddenly across my wrist, wound several times over.

"*Oh, for Goddesses sake,*" I muttered, unraveling the cloth that contained two black eyes and that same little mouth.

I crumpled the bandage, ignoring the muffled cries of the little man it actually was, and inspected my wound.

But I had none.

As I twisted my wrist in the dim glow of the Underrealm, I could not find a wound nor tear nor scar to imply I'd ever fallen and broken it.

"Now, Primordial Goddess so Divine, if I could just take a look at that bleeding hand..." He was back in his Changlingfae form, tugging on the bottom hem of his jacket, which had wrinkled significantly in his transition.

"What is your name?"

A look of surprise lit his face, his large eyes widening even more if that was possible. "Apologies!" He bent at the waist. "I am called Piffle, your most graciously humble servant, Beautiful Goddess so Preternaturally—"

"Reshina will do, Piffle." I rotated my wrist without pain. "And thank you. Your gift of healing is far greater than any I've encountered in the past century. Céad must have been very generous in her gift giving at your birth."

At the mention of the Changlingfae Goddess's name, Piffle uttered a squeak, slapping his hands across his mouth. "The Enchanting Goddess knows Céad?"

"Of course. Did you think one Goddess of the Veil would not know all the others?"

"I-I've spent much time here in the Underrealm as of late. The only other Goddess I've seen is Ishtak!"

A smile curled on my lips. I tilted my head, narrowing my eyes. "You are just the fae I need, then, Piffle. Come, take me to Ishtak and I shall see to it that you see the sun again."

"Beautiful Goddess, I cannot."

"Why?"

"It..." he leaned in closer. "It is forbidden."

"I see," I hummed. "And who is the one who has forbidden one Goddess from meeting with another?"

He shook his head swiftly. "It is not the act of meeting that is forbidden, but the western corridor where she dwells that you must never enter if you wish to...to..."

He held his neck, choking on nothing but air.

I huffed, glancing ahead to where the tunnel ended in a set of stairs. "Don't tire yourself, Piffle. I recognize a man sworn to secrecy by the hand of a Goddess when I see one."

"Th-thank you, My Exquisite—"

"And as I already said once," I added, beginning my steady stride toward the ascending stair, the click of my heeled shoes echoing through the tunnel. "My name is Reshina and you may call me such."

I heard his steps scurrying behind me. "Please! I'll show you to your rooms, Godd—er—Reshina!"

"First," I muttered, swiftly finding the bottom stair, "You will show me the entrance to the western corridor. Then you may show me to my rooms."

"But, Goddess—"

I swiveled on my heel, staring down at the little man in a cold gaze and unfurling my wings at my back. "Do you question a Goddess of the Veil?" My words rang soft and dangerous.

His face scrunched into the shape of a withered squash. "The Master has said—"

I took one calculated step towards him. "A Goddess is your Mistress now, Piffle." I bent at the waist, meeting his eye. "And she takes precedence over any king."

I waited for his confirmation and didn't wait long. A short burst of nods were followed by, "Yes, yes, of course."

"Good. I am happy to follow your lead."

He stepped around me, head bent in submission. "Please do not go there, Mistress. Please say you only wish to see where it is and not to venture."

"Lead the way," I ordered, ignoring his plea and following the little man up the stone stairs and into the heart of the Underrealm.

CHAPTER 7

Arthur

PACING DID ME NO GOOD.

Stretching, examining the spattering of dark bruises across my ribs in the mirror, did me no good either.

Breathing, knocking back a full glass of yagsmead, more pacing—nothing—*nothing* could calm me.

Reshina was here.

Reshina was in the Underrealm.

Reshina was...mine.

But she wasn't.

She never could be.

Another laugh of madness escaped me as I leaned a hand against the tall mirror, catching a glimpse of my deranged state. My eyes of icy blue were bloodshot, yellow hair, dirty and limp down the sides of my face. I followed the line of my scar from the tip of my brow down to the hollow of my cheek.

I hadn't thought of my father in years, but I did then, finding the reflection staring back at me to be a glimpse of the one I'd seen in portraits of him.

Had he been in such turmoil when my mother had bled onto his land? Had he aided in her capture, dragging her below the frozen surface into the dark of the Underrealm?

I had never asked my mother to tell me the details of her part in this curse. Not due to a lack of curiosity, but as a kindness, as she rarely spoke of anything related to her time below the Castle's surface. Of how *I* came to be.

And now, swiping a hand back through my ragged locks, I wished I had. Avoiding the curse hadn't worked, nor had taming the Beast to never draw blood from a woman crossing my lands. Reshina had bled on her own—something I did not take into consideration as a possible outcome. I'd been so careful in the past, avoiding allowing the Beast out if I suspected a woman was above.

My eyes found the Reshina's book, darting to its worn fabric cover, once a deep blue, now almost devoid of color, and frayed at the corners.

I knocked back another glass of yagsmead, the sting hitting my empty stomach. The Beast hadn't eaten his fill, and now I would pay for it with my stomach rumbling in complaint.

I sat on my bed, picking up *The Cursed Goddess of the Veil* from my bedside table. This personal volume was small, easy enough to fit into a jacket pocket, which is where I usually kept it before the curse had come to claim me. Tracing over the debossed title, I thought back to the first time I'd read it. I'd been a young Duke of Riche, practically still a boy at the age of twenty-five, finally having found my freedom away from Heartstone.

Feeling invincible, I traveled throughout Revelry, drinking, gambling, bedding women wherever I roamed—the curse so distant from passing on to me, I forgot about it most days. That first taste of freedom had been everything, but it wasn't until I picked up that book that something else settled into place.

From the moment I'd read the first few pages, I'd been a man obsessed, reading its entirety in one night only to sleep a few hours and pick it up to read again. A strange calm had come over me. I began to see the world differently—through the eyes of a Ravenfae Goddess in her early years, cursed to never feel love.

I stopped attending the parties. Stopped traveling and bringing multiple women to my bed. I'd stopped roaming, instead taking the different fork in the path, reading poetry, taking long walks through the streets of Riche, pondering life and what it meant to love every part of it.

It wasn't until my mother sent word of my father's passing that I returned to Heartstone, the third member of the somber party who attended his funeral. My mother begged me to stay, knowing he had been the reason I'd left. But I had a life as Duke of Riche. I could not abandon the newfound pleasure in living quietly, pretending I was nothing more than a Duke. No curse lying in wait for me.

I opened the cover of *The Cursed Goddess of the Veil*, reading the first line I'd muttered aloud on countless mornings and nights.

> "Once upon a time, a Ravenfae Goddess was cursed to never love another. And though she would live many centuries thereafter, the curse would haunt her for the rest of her days, for how could she ever know what it was to be loved if she was doomed to never return it?"

It was her book that helped me understand what it was to live and love. It was Reshina's story, penned by herself over a century ago, that kept me from going mad in those days, waiting for my mother to die, and for my father's curse to claim me.

And now she was here.

Her blood spilled on my land.

Her life was mine, bound to the land of Heartstone Castle above and the tunnels below. I'd been obsessed with her story for so long, I didn't know how to separate my fixation from the woman I pulled to the Underrealm.

She had glared at me with dismissive irritation as if being brought into the cursed land was nothing more than an inconvenience she'd maneuver herself out of.

She was beautiful.

More Goddess than any other had a right to be called with her powerful wings tipped in silver, her long straight nose and dark hooded eyes. Her lips were red, full and soft. I closed my eyes, picturing her there, settling her into my memory and more than just the Beast inside me marked her as mine.

But she never truly could be.

I had to get her out of here.

Regardless of how much I wanted her to stay.

CHAPTER 8

Reshina

THE UNDERREALM OPENED FROM A DARK TUNNEL INTO A massive hall of stone. Chipped into the walls were creatures of long spindly legs and arms, clawed hands and soulless eyes. They were carved en masse, reaching toward the pinnacle statue at the center of the cavern.

Piffle continued leading the way, oblivious to the sublime of the hall, his little boots echoing with a steady drip of water from somewhere nearby.

The center statue must have been over thirty feet, carved from the same dark stone that I'd fallen through. Torches lined the walls, and I walked across black marble, streaks of white spread throughout.

"Piffle," I said softly, "who is that?"

The little fae turned to me, then back to the statue dominating the hall. "Tis the Master's father, Mistress Reshina."

The heels of my shoes clacked along the stone. "And these creatures?" I stepped closer to the wall, tracing my fingers over the carvings.

"The Mistress has never seen an Underfae before?"

My brows rose. Indeed, I had not. "The Underfae Goddess does not look like her faekind?"

He shrugged. "Do all Goddesses typically?"

"Yes," I replied, frowning. Though Ishtak was a haggard old woman, she did not look like these creatures at least.

"Would…would you like a rest, Mistress? Perhaps a good meal before you settle in for the night? I am a fine cook. Or some tea?" He tugged at my sleeve. "What of some nice hot tea and a good rest?"

"Piffle," I started, taking back my sleeve, "are you trying to distract me from our task at hand?"

"N-no!" He clutched his hands at his chest worriedly. "Yes," he confessed, letting out a breath of air. "It's just that the Master said to take care of you. And reminded me that you are not to venture down the western corridor."

"Piffle," I began again, "would you please point north for me?"

He grinned wide, pointing directly at the monumental statue of the late King of Heartstone.

"Thank you. You may wait here if you wish." I took several steps in the direction of the western tunnel, darker than any other that branched off the great hall.

His tugging on my dress came quicker than I would have liked, and in a flash of irritation, I grabbed ahold of my skirts, yanking them out of his hands.

"Please!" he begged. "You mustn't!"

"Ishtak will not harm me," I said dismissively, picking up my pace. "She cannot. And I will not harm her either."

The little thing could run faster than I'd expected, and as I neared the looming dark, a golden door appeared over the entrance.

Large black eyes popped over the surface and soon thereafter a squat nose and little mouth. "Mistress, you must listen!" the door cried.

I gritted my teeth and crossed my arms. "Are you locked?"

The sound of a locking mechanism clicked through the hall. "Yes."

"Unlock the door, Piffle," I commanded, losing any patience I had left.

"Alright, but hear my warning again, Goddess Divine."

I sighed, keeping my mouth shut, waiting for him to finish his piece.

The golden door cleared its throat. "I cannot say why you mustn't go. But I can say that there is a good reason Master Arthur has forbidden it."

"And what is this very good reason?"

A booming voice echoed across the hall. "A slow death awaits all who enter the western corridor."

I jumped, turning swiftly. The very king I meant to avoid came strolling into the room from one of the eastern tunnels. "Thank you, Piffle, for keeping our guest from entering."

I raised my chin, flaring my wings behind me. "I am a Goddess of the Veil. Whatever you think will harm me, I promise, it will not." I turned away from him, focusing my attention back on the locked door. "Now unlock yourself this instant." The click of the lock resounded and a smile pulled at my lips as I reached for the golden handle.

"Piffle," Arthur snapped, crossing the hall swiftly, "lock the door."

Another click.

"Unlock the door *now*, Piffle," I commanded again, this time my hand already on the handle, ready to open it.

The click came, but the king was ready.

"Lock it, Piffle."

Again a click.

I turned in a flash of anger, finding the king mere inches from me, his hand already reaching for mine.

"You dare use my servant against me?" he growled.

I scoffed in utter disbelief. "*You* dare counter the wishes of a Goddess?"

"This is my realm, not yours. I rule here."

"A Goddess rules everywhere," I fumed, "and the Under-realm is Ishtak's domain, not a king's." I shook my head. "I don't have time for your foolishness." I swatted his hand away. "Remove yourself from this entrance, Piffle."

The door disappeared and the little fae was beside me, worrying his hands again.

Gazing into the utter darkness from the tunnel was like staring into an abyss. Light cast from the torches in the hall fell prey to the hungry mouth of the tunnel's opening, refusing to illuminate more than a few feet within.

"Right," I stated assuredly. "I will speak to Ishtak about this curse and find a way out of it. You may stay here if you wish."

"But Mistress!" Piffle squeaked, slapping his hands over his mouth again.

Arthur's arm blocked my way in an instant. It was massive and straining against his linen shirt as if growing in size right before my eyes.

I furrowed my brow, turning to look at the man.

But he was not a man. Not entirely so.

His chest heaved with the labor of breathing and two horns, black and segmented, pointed out from the top of his head. Twin fangs began to grow down over his lips, and I clucked my tongue.

"Don't tell me you can't control the Beast."

"Only..." he breathed, pausing between words. "When... I'm...angry."

"Ha! Just like a man to not know how to control his temper."

"This *is* control," he growled, closing his eyes with a deep inhale.

"Hardly." I moved to step under his growing arm, but he lowered it.

"The Beast!" Piffle squealed in alarm.

I gave my own growl of frustration, ready to force my way past him.

When I spun to face him, I stopped.

His head, cast in shadow, was half beast, half man, the long scar down his face shining white in the dim glowing light. Eyes of brilliant blue glared back at me.

They held a pain that was rare to see, but one I recognized. I took a good look at him, fascinated by his transformation from man to beast. His yellow hair, soft and curled slightly at the ends, was a direct opposite to the coarse, dark fur sprouting alongside his face and neck.

Giving him a few moments to catch his breath seemed to help as his face began to return to its pale hue, his fangs receding back into his mouth.

"How did you do that?" I asked, curious about his ability to control the curse.

He relaxed, dropping his arm. "The Beast is not easy to control. But if he had been released down here with you..." He scratched his neck where the fur had bloomed. "It would have been worse than anything you'd meet in the western corridor."

"Is that a threat?"

"It's a warning, Goddess. About the Beast and this tunnel." He gestured at the consuming dark. "If you choose to enter, I cannot promise you will come out."

For the first time, I paused at his words. There was very little that could kill a Goddess of the Veil.

Some things.

Some actions.

But few and far between were the fae or humans of the realm who knew of them.

I stared down the hopeless dark. "You cannot tell me why you have forbidden the western corridor?"

"I cannot."

"Because Ishtak has forbidden it?"

"Because when the curse took me, and I spent my first night in the Underrealm, it was the first thing she showed me and the first thing she ensured I would never be able to speak of." He kept his eyes on me, jutting his chin toward Piffle. "Him as well."

It wasn't unheard of for a Goddess to keep her secrets close. I had my own, but whatever it was down that corridor, I sensed the other Goddesses of the Veil would not approve.

I squared my shoulders, raising my chin. "I need to speak with Ishtak."

"I can try to arrange it."

"Good enough," I concluded, adding, "For now. Piffle, you may see me to my rooms. And I'd like that cup of tea as well."

Practically buzzing, he skittered forward. "This way, Your Ravishingness!"

Arthur's brows furrowed at the title and I lifted my lips in a sly smile. "Your servant is quite enthralled, it seems."

I followed Piffle toward a lit corridor to the east, hearing the king mutter behind me, "Aren't we all."

THE UNDERREALM WAS FAR MORE THAN JUST A FEW dank tunnels, as myself and the other Goddesses had been led to believe. In truth, there was no reason for any of us faekind on the surface to venture down into this realm, having no real business nor care for the Underfae. Their existence was simply that.

To exist.

No curses ever came for them beyond the Veil.

No Underfae ever found their way above ground. At least none that I knew of.

Therefore, it unnerved me to walk through the Underrealm, taking in the dark stone arches and pillars carved in intricate patterns. For each turn through the corridors, I became more amazed and bemused. I stopped under a fork in our path that led to three different corridors under ribbed vaulting, astounded at the masterwork of each arched entrance to a new pathway.

"Piffle," I started, "do you know who built all of this?"

He stopped, craning his neck up to the tall vaulted stone ceiling. "It's been like this as long as I've been down here, Mistress."

"And how long has that been?"

He continued on, turning right down a new corridor glowing in soft candlelight. "Since the day you brought the curse to Master Arthur's father, Master André."

"You've been down here for over fifty years?"

He nodded without stopping. "I leave on occasion to gather supplies the Master needs. Ah!" He stopped at a door inlaid into the stone walls. The detailed curvature around the framework must have been from an architectural genius, as on closer inspection, each curve inset into another, detailing vines with pointed thorns.

I traced my fingers along the stone, marveling at the work.

"Does the Mistress like the entrance to her room?"

I jumped back, in a gasp. The question came from a tea cart, or rather, a tea *kettle* with eyes and a mouth.

"Piffle, please...warn me somehow before you change into an inanimate object. It's disorienting."

"Apologies! You are my first guest in many years and...well... the Master is used to my changes by now. I shall do better."

The kettle rose into the air on its own, hovering above a porcelain cup. "Tea?" it asked.

"Yes, thank you."

I pressed on the door latch and stepped inside the room, the rattling wheels of the cart sounding behind me. Before I could mention the dark, flame erupted from the chandelier hanging from more ribbed vaulting at the center of the room.

Along one wall, a massive four poster bed was draped in

luscious deep green linens with plum curtains pulled back at each post. Piles of pillows framed the headboard, carved from dark wood and detailed with varying states of roses in bloom.

I walked across the black marble floor, peeking into the small washing room to see it complete with a sink, stone tub carved into the wall, and all the finest amenities of Revelry above the surface. A massive fireplace took up the wall opposite the bed with a dark purple settee near the fire.

The cart rolled into the room, and Piffle finished the tea pour. I took the cup into my cold hands and sipped it quietly, more questions forming in my mind.

"This is a fine room," I began. "Has it been occupied before?"

Piffle poked at the fire, no longer a cart, but back to his Changlingfae form. "I keep it up to standard."

"Up to whose standard?"

He turned in a flash with a large grin. "Why, the standard of the Master's cursebreaker, of course! Cannot have the woman who was brought to break it live in a dusty old room, now can I? What an embarrassment that would be!" He chuckled to himself, fluffing up a beaded pillow on the couch.

"And...no other has been brought down here as part of the curse?"

"None since the Master's mother."

"Was this her room?"

He shook his head quickly. "The Master has closed off that room. Bad memories and all that. He allows me to keep this one ready."

"Ready for?"

"For the woman who will love him, of course! He is quite Goddessblessed indeed to have captured one who is a Goddess herself!" He darted around the room, adjusting a candlestick here, the corner of a rug there. "Mistress Reshina, I do hope this room is to your liking." He fumbled with his hands again. "I've gathered all the necessary amenities you'll need and with just a few minor color adjustments, I believe you will be most comfortable for your time here."

I exhaled softly, sitting by the fire. "That won't be necessary, Piffle. The color of the room is most agreeable."

"Oh!" he shouted, slapping a hand across his mouth and running to the tall armoire in the corner. "No! I meant for these!" He flung the doors open wide, a rush of brilliantly hued fabric swishing out from behind them. Pinks and pale greens, patterns of florals and shades of sky blue fell from the hooks one by one as he yanked them to the floor. "These would never do, never, never do," he mumbled, gathering the gowns in his hands and tripping more than once as he crossed the room. "Forgive me, Goddess of Beauty, I assumed the Cursebreaker would wear something similar to Mistress Marianna, but, oh! Foolish Piff! These are not for you at all!"

Rubbing a hand across my temple I held in a yawn. "It is not necessary to obtain a new wardrobe as I will not be here long enough to need one." I glanced down to the tears in my black silken skirts and the snags in the lace of my sleeves.

A shame to be sure.

I loved this dress.

"I...I will find you something suitable to sleep in, Mistress. Although I do not see how you could fall in love with the man and that Beast in less than a day, but I am not an expert in such things, either."

"I'll find another way to leave," I said, setting my cup on a small table and bringing my legs up onto the cushions and closing my eyes.

"PILLOW!"

The yell hardly sounded before a stuffed velvet pillow found its way underneath my head, jolting me upwards. "What in the..." I trailed, finding Piffle's face across the golden cushion.

"You said to warn you before I changed. Was that not what

you meant?" it said, slightly muffled and with a bit of stuffing coming from the corner of its mouth.

"What? I—no—" I released a huff of air. "Piffle, I do not need another pillow. I need to lay down for a bit. You may leave now."

He was a fae again, bowing low and backing out of the room. "Of course, Your Radiance! If you need me, you shall only call my name down the hall and I will be with you—"

"Thank you," I interrupted. "That will be all for now."

With an enormous grin, he backed out of the room, closing the door behind him. And with the soft click of the door, I fell across the settee, sleep overtaking me faster than expected.

CHAPTER 9

Arthur

"SHE IS SETTLED, THEN?"

Piff nodded in irritating jubilance. "Indeed! And she said the colors of the room were very agreeable!" He meddled with the pillows along the headboard of my bed, folding back the blankets he'd just worked so hard to tidy. "Those dresses will never do, never ever do," he muttered under his breath. "I'll need to send an order into Riche for darker fabric. Black and perhaps something evergreen, or a deep mulberry wine—"

"Piff," I interrupted, sipping on my fourth glass of yagsmead for the evening. "Reshina cannot break the curse in the way you're hoping she can. I'm sorry to inform you, old friend, but I will be leaving you soon."

"Oh, Master!" he laughed, shaking his head and patting at the sheets. "Your threats don't fool me. You've been at the yagsmead again, and—"

"You don't understand," I rumbled, falling forward with my head in my hands. "Reshina *is* the Cursed Goddess of the Veil. She is cursed to never love another."

"Reshina?" he gasped, picking up her book at my bedside table. "Reshina is..."

"Yes. That book was originally penned by her. To tell her story."

"So you mean—"

"Yes."

"And she can't—"

"She cannot."

"So that means you—"

"Killing me is her only way out of this curse, and it's been a long time coming." I lifted my glass in salute. "It's been a good run, Piff."

"No!" he cried.

"It's how she can leave this mess."

"But! What is her counter curse? What if you break *her* curse and then *she* can break yours!"

I shook my head, sipping the last of my drink. "She's never revealed how to break her own curse. It's been over five hundred years. You'd think she'd have broken it by now if it was easy to do."

He drew nearer, fumbling his hands at his chest. He approached my chair by the fireplace with caution. "Mistress comes looking to speak to Ishtak. Maybe if we made some precautions—"

"I'm not letting her go down the western corridor. Have you forgotten what it was like when I dragged you out of there with me?"

His shoulders shuddered and he pursed his lips. "I remember it, Master. My dreams are filled with those vile things. But if Ishtak can provide some other way to—"

"If I believed she could, I would have trekked down that Goddess-forsaken tunnel as many times as necessary by now." I rose and poured another glass, tipping in the last few drops. Shaking the bottle, I quirked a brow.

"I have more in the pantry, sire. Shall I retrieve another bottle for the night?"

I gulped down the rest. "Make it two. I'd like to offer one to our guest. She'll need it for what I have to tell her."

"Perhaps you could get to know her first? Before you give up and tell her to drive a knife through your heart?"

"I do know her, Piff." I sunk onto my bed, picking up the book. "I've known her story for years."

"That's not the same thing, sire. You know of her origins, her story as Goddess, but you do not know her now—here—as flesh and blood not far from where you sit on that bed."

"It doesn't matter. None of it matters. She could never love me and she never will."

CHAPTER 10

Reshina

WHEN I WOKE, IT WAS A SLOW SLIDE BACK INTO CLARITY. It took me some time to grasp where I was and what had happened. I pressed a palm to my temple, chiding myself at the two glasses of yagsmead I had gulped down at the tavern in Heartstone.

I wandered into the washing room to splash my face with water and swish the taste of sleep from my mouth. Standing at the basin, I sifted through everything that had happened since I bled onto that snow.

The curse of Heartstone Castle had dragged me into it, playing the part of the woman who could end Arthur's curse—the same curse that I had delivered to his father decades ago.

The Underrealm was built by many hands. Fine hands that knew carpentry and masonry. Where were they now? Who had built these vast corridors and that great hall of carved stone monuments?

Ishtak must know. She must retain the knowledge of something that had been lost to time or reason, and more than I needed to quell the rumbling in my stomach, I needed to find her.

My daughter would be leaving for her arranged marriage

within two months, and I needed to help her prepare. There was much to do. She'd need a wedding gown, dresses as a queen, advice on life with a man you did not know—these were the details I could provide my daughter and I intended to.

I slipped into my heeled shoes and clacked loudly across the marble floor, thinking better of wearing them and leaving them beside the bed instead. On bare feet, I lifted the hem of my gown, slipping out the door of my room.

The corridor was still lit, though the hall I slipped quietly down looked exactly like the last. I was soon lost, turning which ways I thought were correct, only to find myself in the same forked path or one that was identical to another. After the seventh turn that led me back to the corridor with my room, I shifted, giving up on legs and flew instead.

When at last I turned down a corridor with a subtle change in the light, I found it opened up into the great marble stone hall. I shifted back into my Ravenfae form, exhausted, angry, and more determined than ever to leave the Underrealm for good. I ran across the black floors, my wings helping to carry me until I stood with cold feet in front of the western corridor.

A breeze shifted toward me, the scent of decay bringing with it a foreboding dread. I shivered but stepped forward, ready to face what might await me in the consuming dark.

The corridor was no more than a roughly paved path through black stone, chipped and jagged enough to pierce my skin if I wasn't careful of my hands and footing. The walls closed in around me as the light from the hall faded away, forcing me to feel my way forward, searching for any sense of light or life.

I walked through the black tunnel, growing colder by the minute and unable to settle my heart with a sense of unease drifting heavily through the air. A clicking sound met my ears and my head snapped up, hitting the edge of a sharp stone.

I cursed in true Goddess fashion and pulled my fingers away from my wound, slipping one into my mouth to taste blood. A drip slid down my forehead, and I wiped it away, scraping my fingers across the wet rocky walls rather than my gown.

The first echo of clicking was soon joined by another, then another, until the clipped sounds resonated through the tunnel, engulfing me completely. They came from ahead and behind, but I continued on, certain that I could face whatever creatures sounded in the dark.

I could not.

The first nip came from the humerus of my left wing—just a pinch, but enough to make me jerk to the right, gasping at the sharp needle-like pain. Still without light, I reached behind my back, brushing at my wing to swipe away whatever it was that bit me.

The second time, it was a piercing bite of sharp teeth at my right shoulder blade, enough to surely draw blood if not flesh ripped from bone. I swiped my arm quicker, hitting something other than rock. The creature clicked as it fell somewhere at my feet with an echoing thump before I was bit again at my ankle, then thigh, then wrist—forcing me to stumble backwards.

Before I could fall, I pulled from my power and swung my arm in an arch, stunning all the creatures in my presence. The biting stopped. The clicking far ahead did not. If I continued, I'd be able to stun dozens at once, but the more I did, the shorter they'd stay still. I stepped over and onto whatever was attacking and turned, racing back down the tunnel as fast as I could towards the entrance, the bites on my skin burning in a fiery rage. The incessant clicking grew and the ominous truth that I would not be able to outrun these creatures came forefront to my mind.

"Ishtak!" I hollered, hoping she could hear me wherever she resided in the corridor. "Please! I need your help!" I stumbled over a jutting rock, cursing as I fell onto my knees, catching myself with my hands just before my face could smack into the hard ground.

"Ishtak!" I cried again, shaking, burning, my wounds on fire, my head throbbing.

A monstrous roar echoed down the corridor and with it, the sound of pounding feet headed straight for me. I had nowhere to go, nowhere to escape the creatures creeping closer and the monster rumbling my way. I tried to shift, seeing it as my only way out of the mess I'd gotten myself into, but the wounds on my skin burned hotter each time I tried. Whatever came from the teeth of those creatures, it was powerful enough to hinder the Goddess of the Ravenfae from the full force of her abilities.

With a deep inhale and shove away from the wall, I chose to run forward, deciding to meet what I suspected would soon find me, rather than face the ravenous creatures behind me, already nipping at my heels.

"I'm here!" I shouted as another roar sounded off the walls, bits of rock tumbling onto my head in its wake. "Arthur! Please!"

Teeth tore at my flesh again, this time enough to take me down where I kicked and fought with everything I had, tearing my own nails into cold, bony bodies, and slamming the creatures as hard as I could into the walls.

I cried out in pain, screaming as one of them leapt onto my chest, biting at my neck with teeth so sharp, I felt my skin rip into ragged strips.

I dug my nails into the creature's spine, yanking it off me when a mass of fur and muscle leapt over my body, tearing into the creatures at my feet. I yelped, backing myself away, whimpering at the sound of flesh and bone crunching under powerful jaws, hearing the sockets popping as limbs were tossed against the walls.

"Mistress!" cried Piffle somewhere behind me, and I turned my head to see a shuddering light, barely illuminating the walls surrounding the massacre happening at my feet.

Squinting in the glow, the only thing I could discern was a

massive form of dark fur, hinged legs and claws sinking into the most disturbing creatures I'd ever seen.

The walls in the great hall did not accurately portray the Underfae that lined the walls of the tunnel. They were no larger than a small child, with spindly arms and legs of gray skin that was so thin, purple and blue veins pulsed throughout. Each had an oversized head with long, needled teeth jutting over purple lips, and black eyes so large, they put Piffle's to shame.

Without hair, each was almost identical to the last, and as the ripping and tearing continued, I found my feet again, backing away straight into Piffle who tried to catch me before falling.

"We must get out!" he cried. "Come, Mistress!"

He tugged and pulled at my skirts, and I began to follow before swinging my arm behind me again, pouring just the right amount of my Cursebringer magic into the scene to freeze as many of the Underfae that I could. I'd meant to stun them all, the Beast included, but my power had no effect on him as he continued to rampage his way through the creatures.

I followed Piffle through the rest of the corridor, the violent scene behind us growing fainter as the light from the great hall grew ahead.

When we stumbled out, I collapsed, turning and scuttling away from the entrance across the cold marble floor. "How do we close it?"

Piffle stood worriedly, holding his torch forward as if to light the way. "They won't follow. They cannot live outside of the dark!"

A booming yelp came from the tunnel followed by a rumble I felt through the floor, sounding off the walls and into the hall.

"Master!" Piffle shouted from a cupped hand, not daring to enter again.

I wiped the blood from my chest, regaining some of my strength, though my wounds were refusing to close. Rising on steady feet, I flew halfway across the hall before my wings faltered. Scraping myself up, I continued on foot, the slap of my bare feet the only sound I could hear.

I didn't care to see what came out of that tunnel—my captor was occupied, and I saw an opportunity to find my way out from the Underrealm. If Arthur was a Beast who roamed the lands above, he must have a way to the surface.

I intended to find it.

I tore through one of the tunnels to the east of the hall, skidding around corner after corner, finding myself lost over and over until I met a set of long stairs rising upwards through the stone walls. Frigid air billowed fresh snow onto the top steps, revealing an entrance to the surface. A solid black door, carved in intricate details, resided opposite the staircase, but I had no time to investigate further.

Before I could look back towards another rumble tearing through the Underrealm, I lifted my skirts and sprinted up the stairs, meeting the surface of Heartstone Castle and a land drenched in white under the silver gaze of the moon.

CHAPTER 11
The Beast

MINE.
RUN.
BLOOD.
CRUNCH.
TEAR.
BONES.
PAIN.
RAGE...GONE.

GONE.
SMELL.
SCENT. CAUGHT.
MINE. RUN.
...HUNT.

CHAPTER 12

Reshina

THE WOUNDS ON MY FEET AND LEGS HAD CLOSED BY THE time I made it to the top of the stairs. The bites across my wings no longer burned, but emitted a dull ache as my body stitched my skin back into place.

I've been through worse, I reminded myself, grimacing in the sting of flesh renewed. Being a Goddess of the Veil came with many ups and downs, but the ability to heal quickly was certainly one of the more useful powers.

I raced through the frozen gardens on feet so frozen, it felt as if I stumbled over hot coals. The gardens were woven into a hedge maze with more twists and turns, like a map of the corridors below. I attempted to shift into a raven once again, but failed, though the ability was still there, just under the surface of my quickly healing wounds.

The moon hung low in the sky and dawn wasn't far off by the looks of it. My lungs heaved out of control, forcing icy air into them to the point of pain, and I took a moment to swallow, gathering my bearings as to where I must be.

With absolute certainty, I knew that stepping outside of the castle grounds would release me from the curse. I just needed to make it there. Gathering my long skirts in my hands, I waded through the snow, frozen down to the marrow of my bones.

Not much further, I told myself, having no real proof that could be true. But I'd learned the power of hope in the most harrowing of times, and I took her hand then, only looking forward, never back.

Until *he* came.

If the bellow of the Beast was heard miles away in the Brackish Wood, I'd have believed it. The ground shuddered, knocking drifts of snow off the tall hedges, but my legs carried me further, faster—away from what I heard burst from the castle behind me.

Run, run, run. I pushed myself, trying over and over to shift and fly away from the madness of the creature who followed me. The boom, the pounding, the uncontrolled rage of a monster sounded dangerously close, and upon a quick glance to gauge his distance, I saw that the hedge maze did not hinder him in the slightest. With each winding path I crossed, he jumped and dove, cutting over the hedges with ease in a straight line to me.

In his full form, he was the most monstrous thing I'd ever seen—with dark fur, massive limbs and black horns curling from the top of his head. No sign of the man I'd met was visible. This creature was all Beast.

And gaining.

Unable to see the end of the maze, I had mere moments to react, ignoring the calls of Piffle somewhere in the distance. I dug my sharp nails into the bite at my chest, seething in pain as I renewed the wound, flicking crimson drops of blood onto the icy layer of snow. Just as I'd hoped, the ground rumbled in protest, shaking and opening in a gap below my feet.

The last thing I saw above the surface was the great jaws of the Beast and the brightest blue eyes of the man he possessed, jumping towards me before I fell down, down, down, underneath the surface of the grounds and back into the Underrealm.

I struggled to grab onto anything to slow my fall, with no room to use my wings and no rock to grip as I fell. I screamed through dirt and stone, root and mud, crashing through the vaulted ceiling of a corridor in the Underrealm.

A crack resounded around me as I landed, and I screamed in pain when my right wing caught the fall, snapping hollow bone and breaking some of my longer primary feathers. I had little time to regain my breath before I was followed, shielding my face with my arm as a large form came tumbling down after me. Bits of rock and dirt rained down before I heard the stones maneuver back into place, sealing the hole as if it had never been.

I peeked over my arm to find the cursed man staring down at me. He didn't touch me, not my skin at least, as his arms were locked at the sides of my head and his legs straddled my hips, pinning my gown to the stone floor. He gulped in heaving breaths, furious and baring his teeth as if the transition from Beast to man was a grueling task.

This close, I was fascinated by the receding fangs and the spiraled horns on his head disappearing back into his bloody, golden hair. He was wounded. Teeth marks littered his skin—circles of red along his neck and chest where his shirt draped in tatters, reforming over his chest as the blood-crusted fur disappeared. His eyes closed and he grimaced in pain, collapsing beside me.

"This," he heaved, "is when I tell you I told you so."

I huffed, rising and wincing. "You did not tell me of *that*," I muttered, gesturing to the bite marks across his neck.

"You shouldn't have been in the western corridor," he snapped, sitting up with me, his eyes darting over my bruised skin.

"You should have warned me better!"

"You should have accepted it's forbidden for a good reason!"

Shaking my head and adjusting my frozen and torn sleeves, I

rose on shaky legs. "Why would I listen to a man who dragged me down here in the first place?"

He bolted to his feet and followed as I began gathering my dignity, refusing to limp, walking through the pain of my broken wing and frozen feet.

"Then you should have listened to the *golden fucking door* blocking your way!"

I hissed a mocking laugh. "I can assure you what I'm *not* listening to is a lecture from *you*."

His hand wrapped around my arm as he turned me to face him. "Oh, you are, Goddess. You're going to listen to every last word I have to say if you're planning to survive down here."

My mouth parted in shock, and I stared at my upper arm where his hand wrapped around it. "You dare put your hands on a Goddess?"

He squeezed, pulling me closer, leaning in where I could hear the rough chords of his voice clearly. "I do. I dare. What do you think you could do to me that's worse than the curse you already bestowed, hmm? What could you do that's more punishment than the fate I'm just waiting for you to deliver?"

I yanked my arm out of his grasp. "And what fate is that?"

His icy glare was just as sharp as mine, tearing into me with his answer. "My death, Goddess. And your freedom."

CHAPTER 13

Arthur

RESHINA'S SCATHING GLARE TWISTED TO CONFUSION. "Your death, my freedom? What in Revelry are you talking about?"

I huffed a short laugh. "You don't remember the conditions that can break this curse?"

"Of course, I do. Your captive must love you as both man and Beast, saying so with true feeling. Something your mother failed to do for your father, apparently."

"No, she didn't love him."

"Or," she continued, "You must die of old age, as I assume your father did, at which point your curse will pass onto your son."

"I don't have a son. Nor can I have children. I made sure of it."

She glanced at my groin then back to my eyes. "You've maimed yourself?"

"Hardly. It's a simple procedure that guarantees I won't be passing this curse on."

She folded her arms, cusping each of her elbows. The stance was regal, reminding me that this woman was used to having power over everyone she met. "I'm not lingering in this forsaken place until you wither and die, Arthur. And I certainly won't be saying the former, so the sooner you get me an audience with—"

"I don't have to die of old age for this curse to break, Reshina."

Her eyes twitched as she narrowed them. "You actually want me to kill you?"

I widened my arms, gesturing to my torn clothes and broken skin. "I'm offering you a simple way out."

"Despite your assumption of my character, you'll find I'm not a Goddess who cares so little for a mortal's life."

"I am far from mortal now."

She cocked her head. "You are human."

A wolfish grin grew across my lips at her confusion. The Beast rumbled that one word again, but I shoved him down. He was weak here in the Underrealm, which was the only reason he didn't emerge as my gaze trekked across the soft candlelight along her skin. I took a step closer, finding that inching myself nearer calmed both the Beast and my aggravation. "I've not been human for the past twelve years, Goddess."

Reshina was a good pretender. I barely caught the slight swallow as her throat bobbed or the way she shifted inward slightly, or the way her heart picked up its pace as I came closer.

"Underfae?" she whispered.

My head moved slowly side-to-side. "Something...new."

Her eyes of rich brown, dark as the frozen earth she'd fallen through, widened. "What are you then?"

Realizing I was inches from her, inhaling her scent, I backed away, shoving my hands in my tattered pockets. "I do not believe it has a name. I've searched the annals of the Underrealm countless times, but the library has been—"

"Library?" she interjected. "Here? Below ground?"

An honest grin washed over me. "Yes," I voiced breathlessly.

"Perhaps I could find something there to get out of this curse another way. Would you show it to—"

"Mistress!"

Piffle came racing around the corner of the corridor, huffing and puffing. "Master! I ran as quickly as I could!"

I cleared my throat, giving even more space between us. "Piffle will see to your wounds. Can I expect to get some sleep? And that you will refrain from venturing down corridors you should not?"

The Changlingfae was already mumbling to himself, stepping around her, looking over her bite marks. She'd healed them well already—most of them no more than circled bruises across her skin, with the exception of the one across her chest that I'd guessed she used to bleed into the snow and escape the Beast. Clever Goddess.

"Don't be ridiculous," she chided, moving out of Piffle's grasp. "I'm already mostly healed. Piffle can attend to you."

"I insist that our guest be taken care of first. I may not look it, but I remain a gentleman."

"Don't be so stubborn."

"I assure you, Goddess, I always will be when it comes to you." I waved my hand, already heading down the corridor. "Piffle, see to her care before you enter my rooms."

"Yes, sire!" he squeaked before shouting, "BANDAGE!"

Golden threads wrapped around Reshina's chest. She clicked her tongue, raising her arms and chiding Piffle.

I chuckled, leaving the scene before she questioned why I wanted to stay. Wandering from one corridor to the next, I found my way back to the door of her room. I stepped inside, picking up the full waxed bottle of yagsmead I'd meant to leave for her before I realized she was gone. I had guessed correctly where she'd wound up.

Ripping paper from the parchment by the writing desk, I wrote her a note.

Consider taking my life as a favor.
Think about it.

I left the bottle and note next to her bed, staying only a moment too long, thinking of pressing my nose into the settee where I scented she'd been for the last few hours. Proud of myself for avoiding the temptation, I stoked her fire and left, shuffling through the halls to my own room behind the great black door at the bottom of the stairs that led to the surface.

Gripping the cold basin of the washing room sink, I inhaled long and slow, looking up into the cracked mirror to see the man she'd seen. Haggard. Unkempt. A thick growth of hair across my chin, jaw, and neck—I hadn't bothered to shave in the days before she came, and now, as I rubbed at the scruff, I thought it might be time to consider my appearance for a change.

Once, long ago, I found myself to be an attractive man.

But now... I splashed water on my face, breathing into a fresh towel Piffle had left me. Now, all I saw was the remains of a Beast. A man not thoroughly human, but a monster's disguise staring back at me.

I wiped at my scar, remembering the day my father had given it to me. The curse had always been so far away, always something that was his problem to deal with, not mine. How foolish and young I'd been back then. How naive was that man, certain the future his father had faced did not belong to him.

MINE.

The voice was my own, but dark, broken...sure.

I'd learned to separate myself from the Beast these past twelve years, but having Reshina here, I felt us colliding with the same goal.

I knew so much of her life and she knew nothing of mine.

I was nothing to her—just an annoyance, a mark in her long life to sometimes remember but mostly forget.

MINE.

The rumble came again and I left the mirror, no longer wishing to see the man I'd become, who craved this woman.

Who wanted this woman.

Who would consume this woman given the slightest chance.

My obsession with Reshina, the Goddess of the Ravenfae, had begun long before the Beast took me. But I hoped it would end with my last breath and a dagger from her hand into my heart.

CHAPTER 14

Reshina

IN SILENT CURIOSITY, I ALLOWED PIFFLE TO HEAL THE rest of my wounds. I'd been sent to the Underrealm for less than a day and I'd learned so much in that time. I needed to settle. To think.

I tested my shift into a raven a few times before I was satisfied that I was not permanently damaged, and after leaving my rooms for less than five minutes, the Changelingfae brought me a sleeping gown of deep emerald silk along with a black robe cuffed in black lace. I wondered where he'd gotten it on such short notice of my arrival, but was too exhausted to ask, my body needing rest to renew the power I'd spent stunning the Underfae and healing from their teeth marks.

"Piffle," I started absently, brushing the tangles from my long black hair. "What more can you tell me about the Underfae?"

He shuddered, fluffing up the pillows across my bed. "You know what I know, Mistress. They need the dark. They take their sustenance...through..." His black eyes widened for dramatic effect as he finished. "...*blood.*"

"And they've always been this way?"

He shrugged. "They have since Master André's curse. I've been here at least as long as that." He finished the last pillow and folded the sheets back. "Please say you'll not go back. Please promise, Mistress. Not just for your sake, but for the Master's." Sighing heavily, he took my hand as if I were a child, leading me to the bed, pulling the covers over me as I slipped inside. "If you wander down the western corridor again, he will follow. He will always follow you."

"Always?" I questioned, covering a yawn.

He nodded vigorously. "Now that you are bound as his captive to this curse, the Beast will follow if ever you are in danger. Or if ever you try to leave his lands. Or if ever you do something to make him truly angry. Or if ever you—"

"The Beast will always follow me if I get to the surface?"

"Yes, Mistress. He will be called by the curse to drag you back, so do be careful." He shook his head, blowing out the candles around the room. "You are relatively safe from the Beast here in the Underrealm, but anywhere on the grounds above... he will come for you."

Fascinated, I remained silent, thinking through how I could test Piffle's assertion.

"Goodnight, Elegant Goddess. Shall I wake you in the morning with tea and breakfast?"

"Yes, Piffle, thank you," I murmured, turning across the soft silken sheets, my eyes already fluttering to a close, my mind already formulating ways I could escape the binds of this curse —for one curse upon my soul was more than enough.

CHAPTER 15
The Beast

NOT HERE.

She's sleeping.

MINE.

Incorrect.

WANT BRINGER.

Yes, I know. If you're going to just wander in the cold shouting "MINE" over and over, you might as well relinquish yourself to me and let me sleep below.

NO.

Then find something to hunt already. At this rate, I'll be asleep the entire day and won't even get to see her.

HUNGER.

Then eat, you dolt.

NOT FOR DEER.

Go find where she bled in the snow. That will satisfy you for now.

SCENT.

FOUND.

SWEET.

I don't doubt it. Settle in, Beast. It's been a long night.

SLEEP NEAR BRINGER.

Absolutely not.

YES.

No.

YES.

Goddessdamn you! If you lay a single claw on her, so help me—

JUST SLEEP.

...Alright. Just this once. I'll show you the way if you promise to be gone by the time she wakes.

MINE.

No. But perhaps our savior, my friend.

CHAPTER 16

Reshina

SLEEP TOOK ME, BUT NOT FOR LONG. I HADN'T BEEN ABLE to sleep more than a few hours at a time for a few centuries, and even though I'd been dragged into the Underrealm, attacked by creatures I had no knowledge existed, and had barely escaped the jaws of a monstrous Beast, I woke just two hours after my eyes closed for the night.

Dawn was approaching according to the tall clock near the fireplace. After preparing myself for my tasks of the day, I donned the single gown Piffle had left in the wardrobe.

It was a deep sapphire blue—a color I rarely wore, but I could at least pretend to like instead of one of those pink rosebud pieces he'd rightfully pulled from their hangers. The neckline cut a square at my chest and the sleeves ended at my elbows, cascading into a black lace frill. I yanked the corset ties out of the back, making space for my wings—another adjustment I'd have to mention to Piffle. I shoved the strings into my pocket. For now, the top of the dress would stay, but I'd need Piffle's help to add the strings back into their loops if I planned to keep the dress from falling off my chest throughout the day.

I pinned my thick black hair into a knot on top of my head,

adjusting my crown of silver and black branches, and slipped on my black heeled shoes.

I wanted to find my way back to that staircase, investigate the black door, and find the library Arthur had mentioned—all before Piffle came to wake me in two more hours. I'd need to be quick and quiet.

Pressing on the door handle, it opened a crack before hitting something lumped behind it. Not furniture, but something with give. I shut the door, trying again with more force, only to hear a mumbling of curses on the other side.

With enough room to slip through, I frowned at the man lingering on the stone tiles. "Why are you lying outside of my door, Arthur?"

He wore the same clothing as the night before—ripped shirt, bare feet, bites turned to mostly healed bruises by Piffle's attendance no doubt.

"I meant to leave before you woke," he grumbled, sitting up and rubbing his face.

"That doesn't explain why you are here in the first place," I huffed. "Let me assure you, I am in no hurry to return to the western corridor anytime soon."

He pushed on the door to stand upright. "It wasn't that."

I slipped my hands into the pockets of my gown—its best feature by far. I played with the corset strings and little vials of curses I always carried, my anger at my situation getting the better of me. "What then? Do you lack a bed in these tunnels somewhere?"

Adjusting his shirt and pulling at the tears, he hummed low. "Of course I have a bed."

Getting nowhere, I changed the subject. "Piffle tells me I am only safe from the Beast if I'm here in the Underrealm. Is that true?"

"Piffle talks too much."

"At least he talks to me at all."

"Did you get my note?" he asked, ignoring my question.

"Yes."

"And?"

I shook my head, turning down the hall, already done with him. "I'm not killing you, Arthur."

His steps echoed behind me. "You'll find it's the only way. You have a family. Children. A life. I have nothing but this place. The sooner you choose to end me, the better the outcome for the both of us."

I spun on my heel. "To take a life would be detrimental to mine. Even I have limits. I will find another way out."

A muscle ticked across his sharp jaw, flexing the long scar down his face—something I'd been curious about since I first saw him. "The only way you're leaving here is by killing me. Because we both know you'll never say the words, 'I love you'. It will be a maddening next hundred years for you, Reshina."

"Your father did not live for hundreds of years before the curse was lifted from your mother."

"My father was not bitten by the Underfae."

"What does that mean?"

"It changed me," he added casually. "Now turn around. I'll string this for you."

He pulled at the black corset ties hanging out of my pocket, turning my shoulders so my back faced him. I was too surprised by his insinuation to resist as I felt the tug of his fingers pulling the strings through the eyelets.

I looked over my shoulder to catch a glimpse of his bruises again. "You've been bitten by the Underfae before last night?"

"Yes. The first night the curse took me, I hunted for Ishtak, same as you. I would have been bled dry by those things if not for the Beast taking over." With swift hands, he pulled and adjusted the laces, careful not to pinch my wings. "But in the end, their bites changed me. Now I don't know what I am."

I glanced at my arms. Not a single mark was left from the frenzy the night before. "I feel no different."

"I don't know if faekind are affected in such a way. Or if a Goddess could ever change. I only know that I have ceased to be human for some time now."

"And what?" I huffed, allowing his hands to turn me again at the waist when he was finished. "You believe you'll live on with this curse for centuries because you were bitten by those creatures?"

"Reshina," he whispered, stepping closer, "I have not aged since that day."

I quickly scanned him again. By my understanding, he should be through about half of a human life. But he did not look it. Humans aged dramatically—wrinkling, slowing down—their few decades in this realm changing them so quickly, it felt like the blink of an eye before one passed over to the Veil and thousands more were born.

But Arthur didn't look to have lived much beyond his fourth decade of life. His forehead held a few lines from worry. His eyes and mouth showed little residual evidence of a life of smiles and laughter. He could be as old as I was when I stopped showing signs of age at thirty-seven. It was a common time for faekind to cease aging until they reached over a thousand years old, something I would not achieve for a few centuries yet.

"These...creatures. You're sure they're Ishtak's Underfae?" I asked with caution.

"I..." he began, swallowing in distaste. "I cannot say... particulars..."

Sighing, I shook my head. "Don't strain yourself. I recognize a Goddess's bind when I see it. I'd like you to take me to the library, but first..." I looked him over again. Dark circles under his eyes told me he hadn't slept much. The slump of his wide shoulders confirmed it even more. "I'd like to try to leave. Again. Before I commit to finding another way out of here."

A grin tugged on his lips. "What do you have in mind, Goddess? The Beast will always capture you before you leave the grounds. And he's known for his insatiable desire for blood." He stepped even closer—close enough that I was forced to step one foot behind me to keep my balance. "He is certainly yearning for a true taste of yours."

"How does it work, exactly? If you're locked in chains down here, could I get away before he could break through them? Could we try it?"

"Sure, I keep a set of chains in my rooms."

I laughed. "Do you really?"

"No," he said swiftly. "I left them at my home in Riche before my mother died and left me to become the Beast she hated."

I folded my arms across my chest. "Typical, for a son to blame his mother for something she could not change."

"I don't blame her," he growled. "I blame you."

"Ah," I said, turning down the corridor. "A much better choice as I am used to the blame for the title forced upon me. As if I had any other choice but to deliver those curses."

He dashed to my side, walking with me. "But your son bears the title of Cursebringer now. So you have done what my mother did. You've passed the burden onto your child."

I shook my head. "Not that you would understand, but Korven took the title for himself. He trained for many years to take it in his sister's place. He wanted it to save her from the burden."

"Yes," he grumbled. "He does play the overprotective part well."

I stopped in my tracks. "You've met?"

He tilted his head side to side. "I like to think I aided him in pursuing what he truly desired."

"You're friends?"

He laughed, the boom reverberating in the hall and flickering the low candlelight. "Your son loathes me. That I am sure of. Almost tossed me out a window once."

My frown deepened. "Well, regardless, it's fine that you blame me. Hate me all you want, I—"

He darted in front of me, blocking my way. "I don't hate you, Reshina. Blame and hate are not synonymous here."

"I'd hate me," I said softly. "I don't mind if you do."

His head shook slowly. "It's more complicated than that. Your deliverance of this curse altered the course of my life forever. But I only exist *because* you delivered this curse. I lived a full life before the call of the Beast took me." He stepped closer, towering over me and blocking the light. "I am ready to die. I avoided trapping another down here for over a decade, but when I realized it was you...this is how the curse was meant to be broken. With your knife in my chest." He laughed lightly. "A sort of cruel twist on Cursebringer, don't you think? To first bring the curse and then be the one to end it."

"And what?" I breathed, easing into the space between us. "Am I to live with the guilt of taking your life for the rest of my days? Not to mention the punishment that would follow for stealing a life from the Veil before its time? I'm not your escape, Arthur."

"I beg to differ," he growled. His eyes were ice—such a cold blue, I swear I had not seen a color that could compare. "Do it." He jerked his head toward the end of the corridor where it met a forked path. "Run. Let's see how far you make it before the Beast cuts into your flesh and drags you back underground. Escape is not an option, Goddess."

I shivered at the offer, something stirring in my chest at his words. "And if I do, you'll stay here for as long as he lets you?"

"Yes."

I stepped around him, heading down the hall. "I don't know the way to the stairs."

"Feel the pull. Know what you desire and the halls will show you the way."

"Alright," I said warily.

"Run," he commanded again.

I shook my head with an easy grin. "No, Arthur, I shall fly."

I shifted, soaring away, searching for that pull he spoke of.

The stairs, the stairs, I thought over and over, coming to the two paths. I veered right, not sure I felt anything in particular—it was just the first thought I had.

Not a sound came from behind me, and I hoped that meant Arthur would keep his word and stay in the Underrealm as long as he could. Surely the Beast could not catch a raven.

Surely, this was my chance at escape.

CHAPTER 17

Arthur

PACING DID LITTLE TO HOLD HIM BACK.

As soon as the challenge was issued, the Beast began to rattle his cage.

Just hearing her say *Beast* caused a riot within my chest, and the civility of the gentleman I once was became impossible to find again. Reshina had been under this curse for a little over a day and she was already driving me to madness.

OUT.

"Not yet," I seethed between gritted teeth, flexing the fingers that had tied up her dress. The Beast could not leave the confines of the castle grounds, so if Reshina left them...perhaps she truly could escape this curse and leave me to rot here for all time.

HUNT BRINGER.

"*Wait*," I urged, my arms spread wide over the stone wall, my head falling, breathing, sweating, giving her as much time as I could before she was hunted down.

BLOOD. HUNGER. MINE.

The shift came as I felt her spirit, tied to mine, soar into the winter air. In the next moment, I was no longer a man, but a Beast with a man trapped inside, raging through the corridor, leaving claw marks across the stone as the monster rounded the corner faster than should be possible.

Get out, get away, I thought with no control over anything that would happen next. The Beast skidded across the halls, knocking into Piffle on his way to the kitchen.

"Master!" he yelped, but the Beast did not heed his cries, finding the staircase in record time, sniffing the air when the cold hit above the Underrealm.

I could see glimpses of what the Beast saw, but I could not easily control him, only occasionally able to convince him of one decision or another. He looked up to the sky, exhaling enormous puffs of air, uncharacteristically not speaking to me, instead focused like the hunter he was.

Finding his target, I caught a glimpse of black wings against a dawning horizon. The pounding of his feet rumbled the earth. The scraping of his claws over the hedges filled the air. He sprinted past the marble statues—once an adornment to the castle, now broken monuments to a broken kingdom.

She neared the iron fence around the boundary of Heartstone Castle, and the Beast picked up speed, one word echoing in that all-consuming growl.

MINE.

Faster. She'd need to be faster if she was to make it, for the Beast now leapt beyond the limits of any creature of the realm, picking up speed instead of losing it. She grew tired—her flight dropping, her speed slowing. The Beast's roar boomed as, with one final leap, he secured his prey.

"*Do not harm her!*" I bellowed in his head.

He'd trapped her near the edge of the grounds. Pinned in fresh snow, she shifted back into her Ravenfae form. The Beast's claws dug into her wings spread out behind her. For the first time, she looked frightened, her breath coming in milky white puffs of air as she looked up into the face of a monster.

"*Take her down and be done with this,*" I commanded.

The Beast didn't bother to respond, instead dragging his tongue across her chest, tasting, marking—and I knew what came next.

"*STOP!*" I ordered, urging myself to say it even though I wanted it just as much as he did.

She strained under his form and screamed into the frozen air as the Beast's fangs dug into her neck, spilling her blood onto the snow.

CHAPTER 18

Reshina

PAIN RIPPLED THROUGH ME AS I BLED FOR A THIRD TIME onto this cursed land, the flesh along my neck tearing, followed by the tongue of a monster.

We fell together, down, down, down into the horrid stench of earth, long since seen the sun. Past the rocks and roots, into the stone walled corridors of the labyrinth within the Underrealm.

The pain of the fall was nothing compared to the fire burning across my skin and the resounding crack of my collar bone. Sharp fangs tore one last rip across my flesh before the mouth of a man traveled along the wound, sucking, nibbling, moaning into my skin, flayed and broken.

I panted through the throbbing, knowing I should push him away, aware that he was the one who had done this to me. But his mouth soothed the fire in my veins. The stinging pain of the Beast's fangs, snapping my bone so clean, grew numb with Arthur's tongue passing over my skin, gentle, and caressing.

My breathing eased and I opened my eyes, blinking away the bits of dirt. "Please," I whispered, unsure if it was a plead for him to leave or stay.

When he lifted his head, his eyes of the palest blue caught mine and he seemed to realize what he had done. He bolted from me, backing up against the wall, wiping my blood from his lips. "I'm sorry," he said quickly. "I'm sorry. Are you—"

He reached out a hand and I flinched away, sheltering my broken collar bone. "You were right," I panted. "I didn't make it."

"I cannot control the Beast, Reshina. I tried to give you as much time as I could, and I tried to stop him, but...it's now your blood he craves."

I stood on shaky legs. "You as well?"

His lips parted, but he didn't speak, shaking his head.

"Whatever you just did, it numbed the pain. The Beast's bite was...excruciating. But your mouth—"

"I don't know why," he rasped. "I've never done that before." He straightened his shoulders, adding, "Come. I'll see you to your rooms where Piff can heal you and get you something to eat."

I followed him in silence down the corridor, using the walls to keep myself upright, planning through my next attempt at escape. I wasn't fast enough this time, but if I flew higher in the sky and then across the grounds, I might have a better chance. Though the last leap of the Beast before he caught me was impossibly high, as if he was flying himself.

I wasn't giving up. I wasn't even close.

Once I healed, I'd try again.

And again.

Until I got out of this curse the only acceptable way I could.

PIFFLE TSKED FOR THE TENTH TIME, FUSSING OVER THE state of my neck, not to mention the state of my dress.

He shook it out after I had changed back into my nightgown,

ready to take a rest after a heavy breakfast of sausage, toast, and porridge.

"The Mistress will have to wait until morning before I can bring another gown. I've already started, you see, but with the interruption and tending to that nasty bite, I've not had the time to—"

"It's alright, Piffle, thank you," I yawned, feeling flushed, peeking under the new bandage over my wound. When he'd attempted to heal it, the bone had snapped painfully back into place but the teethmarks remained, pulsing and red. I told myself I just needed some rest and that when I woke, I'd see nothing but a slight bruise.

"PITCHER!" he yelled before popping into a golden container full of cool water, refilling my glass by the bedside table.

I only jumped a little that time and sunk under the bedsheets, exhausted and more than slightly dizzy. "Wake me in two hours if I'm not up already."

He popped back into the shape of a Changlingfae, pulling the sheets up over my shoulders. "Yes, Mistress Reshina. I'll leave you to rest then and work on your garment. I must ask—do you prefer beads or jewels on your corset?"

"Both," I murmured, finding sleep overtake me.

I DREAMED OF THE COLD.

I lay over frozen earth, the icy chill at my back encasing each feather in a prison of sharp frost. But it was a dichotomous place.

Though my wings were frozen in place, my chest, my thighs, my neck were warm—*hot*—burning with a soothing touch that could only come from the bare skin of one meeting the bare skin of another.

The wound on my neck began to pulse, my heart timed to the same beat. A creature covered me, moving slowly, luxuriously—that languid place of enjoying the fruit of the flesh with all the time in the world to consume it.

I couldn't see who it was, only feel, my eyes blinking rapidly, trying to wake, but trying so hard to stay.

And with one gasp and shudder, teeth dug back into my skin, igniting my body in fire, melting the ice at my back and whispering one word into my ear.

Mine.

CHAPTER 19

Arthur

"No," I growled, pacing in front of Reshina's door.

"But, Master!" Piff cried, lifting the plate of beef liver covered in some sort of onion and mushroom gravy. "She requested I wake her! And she needs food to replenish the blood you—*the Beast*—took from her!"

"I gave my order. You're not waking her."

His face crumpled into the fiercest frown I'd ever seen. He set the tray on the ground, stomping his foot. "At least let me check her wound. You owe her that."

"No," I said simply, continuing to wear out the stone in front of her door. "I won't risk you waking her. She's healed fine before."

Piff twisted his lips to the side. "This wound was...different."

I raised a brow.

"It's...not...healing from my magic."

"WHAT!" I roared, slamming the door open, breaking its hinges.

"Master!" he squealed, following at my heels. "You'll frighten her awake!"

Knowing he was correct, I gritted my teeth instead of demanding she wake and show me the bite. It took just a few steps to get to her side, but I knew something was off from the moment I saw her. Her body tossed in the sheets of deep green, sweat beading across her forehead, plastering her long dark hair to her face.

The moment I got to her side, she groaned, her chest heaving. I gently touched her forehead. "She's burning up," I said softly as Piff climbed up next to her other side, peeling back the bandage over her wound.

The puncture was a bright crimson, the skin around the holes swollen far more than they had been when I'd left her at her door.

"Piff," I muttered, and he changed immediately into a golden jar of salve in my hand. I used two fingers to scoop the paste, gently spreading a thin layer over the marks. She groaned again, tossing her head about.

"Fetch a cool cloth," I ordered next and Piff popped back into a man, scurrying to the washing room. I pressed the cloth across her forehead, already feeling the heat rise through it.

"What is this?" I asked the Beast, waking him from his slumber deep within me.

MINE.

I growled in frustration. "What is this wound you've given her? It's infected. What have you done?"

BRINGER HEAL. FROM YOU.

"How?" I gritted, holding onto what little patience I had left.

I BITE. YOU SOOTHE.

"Fuck," I muttered. "Piff, this is worse than I thought."

He was back on the bed, changing out the cloth across her forehead. "What did the Beast say?"

"He said I need to soothe the bite."

"But how, Master?"

I gave him a wry look, his frown following before he slapped his hands across his lips. "You don't mean..." he started.

I nodded, peeling the sweat soaked hair from her face. Her

beauty could not be denied, even as she fought a fever delivered by the monster inside me.

What could kill a Goddess?

A bite from the Beast she'd brought beyond the Veil?

I couldn't imagine so, but I'd been through stranger things in my life than what I needed to do. I wanted to touch her. That truth was clear and had been the moment I'd confirmed it was she who fell into my realm. But more than touch, I wanted my mouth on her skin, breathing into her and taking a moment, no matter how small, to possess her.

I bent lower, salivating just looking at her wound. I chose to write that off as a remnant of the Beast's desire for blood more than my own.

When my lips pressed over the bite mark, she stirred, but in a different way. As my tongue traced over her, gentle, like a lover, she gasped, moaning and lifting her torso in the sheets. My body reacted with nothing short of lust, shaming me as she lay battered and bruised. She sighed as I sucked and licked, her heavy breathing soothing into something languid. Her heart slowed and her head stilled as she slipped into a deep slumber.

It was difficult to pull away—I wouldn't deny it—and as I replaced the bandage, I savored the taste of her skin on my tongue.

"Master," Piffle whispered, and I jumped, startled to remember he was there. "She is calm and sleeping. I will stay with her—"

"No," I growled, clearing my throat and pulling a chair to her bedside. "I will stay. The Beast rests—she is in no danger. I will call for you if I'm in need of your assistance."

He slid off the bed. "I will check back in an hour."

I nodded silently, watching the soft rise and fall of her chest as the Changlingfae left Reshina to sleep and me to my thoughts, dark as ever in the crackling firelight.

CHAPTER 20

Reshina

FIRE FLARED ACROSS MY NECK AS I WOKE, BLINKING rapidly in the soft light. I was in my room below ground. Heat radiated from my wound, burning my skin. I traced my fingers across the bite, surprised to find the bandage gone.

"How much does it hurt?"

The voice was Arthur's and with more blinking, his form took shape. He sat on a chair beside my bed, his head resting on his fist with over a day's worth of hair growth stubbled over his chin. His brow furrowed, his mouth upturned into a frown, and his gaze...something akin to sorrow crossed it.

I pulled myself upright, pressing at the tender bite that had somehow not healed over in my sleep. "It is painful," I rasped. I brought my hand to my mouth, my tongue dry and solidly foul.

Arthur rose, offering a cup to my lips. I tried to swat him away and take it for myself, but my hands shook, so I accepted his help in frustrated silence.

When I'd had a few gulps, he took it from my lips to refill. "You've been asleep for two days."

I closed my eyes, promising myself it would be for just a moment. "That's not possible," I managed to speak, reaching for the cup of water again.

After he helped me take more sips, I slumped back down into the bed, altogether exhausted and in such confusion, the blissful ignorance of sleep drew me closer.

"Reshina," he whispered somewhere near my face.

"Hmm?"

"You cannot fall back to sleep. I need you to eat, then you can rest some more."

I lifted my hand, feeling for him. With a dreamy hum, I remembered this face. It was the same one from my dream of heat and ice and skin. I traced a finger down his nose, following the soft curve, the dip above his lips.

"Reshina," he repeated, this time with a sigh and a press of his cheek into my palm.

"It doesn't hurt when I sleep," I mumbled, dropping my hand and drifting back to the fading black.

I WOKE AGAIN WITH NO PAIN AT ALL, THOUGH THERE WAS a heaviness across my body. Arthur breathed against my skin, the heat tracing over my wound and soothing it with each puff of air. He slept with his forehead pressed to my temple, his arm draped across my belly, fingers tucked around my waist. It was warm and comfortable. A place I could stay for a little while before he woke and I had to pull away again.

It wasn't that I cared for him.

It was that the bite of loneliness over six hundred years was a bite he could soothe in that moment, holding onto me as if we were lovers. As if we knew the intimacies of each other and had taken a moment to say through our bodies, *you are not alone.*

I watched as his light lashes flickered, his eyes opening

slowly, finding mine. He didn't say a word. Didn't move, didn't release me. He just stared. And I stared right back.

The clattering wheels of a teacart slid into the room, along with the clink of a porcelain cup on a saucer. Arthur was the first to break the trance between us, rising from the bed and stepping away to join Piffle somewhere in the middle of the enormous room.

I attempted to do the same, but couldn't manage any more than to pull myself up higher on my pillow, exhausted from the tips of my fingers to my toes in the effort.

Arthur and Piffle whispered together near the foot of my bed, but I could not make out their words as I began to drift again.

"Mistress," Piffle whispered near my head. "I've made some broth to soothe your stomach and regain your strength. Can you sit up just a little more?"

I shook my head with effort. "Where..." my voice caught in my throat. "Where is Arthur?"

"Gone, Mistress. The Beast has not been let out for three days and...he is struggling to contain him. Take just a sip for me."

He held a spoon at my lips and I opened my mouth. A warm broth, salty and ripe with roasted garlic, trickled across my tongue. I took several more spoonfuls, listening to Piffle's explanation of how worried he'd been and how many gowns he'd made.

"Another is a green silk. Leftover fabric from these sheets! I draped this one so it falls across your waist and gathers at your hip with a cascade of shiny black beads I found at the Heartstone market last year."

"Piffle," I croaked, able to lift myself a little higher in the bed. "What time is it?"

"POCKET WATCH!" he hollered, shifting into a golden circle and chain complete with eyes and a mouth.

An endearing grin tugged at my lips as I picked him up, pushing on the clasp to read the time. "It's nearly midnight."

He popped back into a fae and took the bowl and spoon back to the cart. "Yes, much to do, much to do," he muttered, clattering the dishes.

After he helped me to the washing room, where I managed to scrub my face and rinse my mouth, I slowly got back into bed, turning on my side. My body was sore and the broth had begun to lull me to sleep again. My wound throbbed, but not nearly as much as it had days before. I supposed I had Arthur to both blame and thank for that.

"I will see you in the morning," I murmured. "Thank you for your help. Could you—" I cut myself off, deciding not to ask for Arthur to return.

"Mistress?"

"Never mind. Goodnight, Piffle."

"Goodnight, Goddess So Sublime," he whispered, leaving the room and leaving me to fade into the dark once more.

CHAPTER 21

The Beast

IT IS TIME TO RETURN.

NO.

You've been out here for thirteen hours. Your time is over.

YOU STEAL TIME.

She needed me. I had to stay with her.

I BITE. YOU SOOTHE.

Yes, you told me that. It worked. I need to check on her.

LITTLE MAN CHECK.

Piffle's magic is not healing that wound correctly. What if she's in pain?

PAIN GOOD. BLOOD GOOD.

You're impossible to reason with when you get like this. The sooner I help get her back in good health, the sooner she'll try to escape again, and the sooner you can catch her.

...BRINGER RUN?

Yes, she will try to run again. But I need to see her and help get her back to full strength.

YOU NEED BRINGER.

I need to assess—

NO. YOU NEED BRINGER. I GET HER FOR YOU. I BITE SO SHE NEED YOU.

You knew she would need me?

I GET BRINGER FOR *US*. ME, BLOOD. YOU…

Me?

YOU FIND OUT.

That's very cryptic of you.

ONE MORE KILL.

Make it quick. I need to see her.

YOU LET ME OUT TOMORROW?

Yes.

SWEAR ON HER.

Fine. I swear.

I CHANGED INTO SOMETHING LESS RAGGED, LESS covered in sweat and blood before heading to Reshina's room. It was late—past two in the morning, but I just needed to see that her fever wasn't raging again before I'd be able to get some sleep.

I knocked softly on the door before entering. Piffle jerked awake in the chair at her bedside, quickly bolting from it to meet me at the door. I entered quietly, shutting the door behind me. Reshina was asleep in her bed, but still, which was a good sign.

"How is she?"

"She is better. She was awake two hours ago. Drank some broth and got washed up. She was asking about you."

"Did she say she was in pain?"

He shook his head quickly. "No, but I doubt she would have admitted it if she was." He glanced over his shoulder at the bed where she turned. "That bite would have killed any other. We've never seen what the Beast's bite can do to anything but a wild animal." His eyes crinkled in a wide grin. "I believe you saved her, Master."

"I'm also the one who almost killed her."

"Well," he started, gathering the half-finished gown draped across the settee. "You did warn her about the Beast. And you are not him. So my reasoning stands more true than yours. You saved a Goddess's life. That's got to be good for something in your future."

I sighed heavily, following the pull to her side. I fell into the chair by her bed, looking over the wound. In three days it had healed quickly, but the puncture wounds remained, albeit shriveled into mere pinpricks. Disappointment settled into my chest. She wouldn't need me like she had for the past few days when I'd kept her fever at bay. She wouldn't need my mouth on her any longer, and I was a bastard for wanting her to.

"There's a bit of bread and butter on the cart if you're hungry. I'd like to get some rest myself before the day begins if you'll stay—"

"Go. I've got it from here. Thank you, Piffle."

"Her gown," he said, patting at another bundle of fabric I hadn't noticed. "If she would like to dress before I've returned."

I waved him away, running my fingers through my hair.

After he left, I crawled into the bed.

I'd get one more night, *Goddess help me*.

I settled in beside her, careful not to jostle her too much and wake to what I was sure would be the wrath of a Goddess.

Her skin had paled in the three days she'd fought the Beast's bite, but as I brought my arm back around her waist again, pulling her to me, a flush of pink rose on her cheeks. I huffed heavily out of my nose, warming her skin and she hummed in return, still in her dreams where I could not get to her.

"*Reshina*," I whispered softly, placing my mouth over her wound one more time. Her body turned into mine as my lips traced over her skin.

She'd hate me come morning.

Hate I could handle.

Losing her, I couldn't and never would.

I wondered, watching her chest rise and fall, if she dreamt of her life. Of her past lovers tracing their mouths over her skin, or if it was me she saw in her dreams.

I was a man who'd been intrigued by her story for decades.

And now, I was a man obsessed.

And obsession was the exact reason my death was the best option. For both our sakes.

Reshina

"THIS MATERIAL IS DIVINE, PIFFLE. WHERE DID YOU COME across something like this so quickly?" I admired the fit in the long washing room mirror. The fabric was a soft black velvet embroidered in hundreds of wine red rose buds. It fit better than anything I'd made or commissioned myself, and with the slight drape of the long sleeves at my wrist, I wondered if Piffle had measured all parts of me in my sleep.

"When I saw it last year, I knew I must have it," he said with giddiness. "It was the first dress I got to work on right away. Two more are almost finished, including one I think the Master will–"

"Where is Arthur?" I interrupted, sitting to pin my hair into my crown. The effort made my arms weak, and I had to stop with it halfway atop my head. Four days of rest and nothing but sips of broth had brought me to an exhaustion I'd never experienced before.

"He's up there," Piffle said casually, pointing toward the vaulted ceiling. "He wants to show you something today if you're up for it. He's just getting some things ready."

"Something above the surface?"

"No. Something for you to do."

I took the cup of tea he handed me, sipping and contemplating my next moves. Once my strength returned, I could attempt my escape again. Five days wasn't too long of time lost and Morella would soon be visiting her brother anyway. Neither of my children were ever too concerned about my lengths of absence, nor were they in need of me in that time. They had each other—I'd made sure of it.

If I could get away from the grounds within the next two weeks, I'd at least be able to see Morella off before her marriage. And as long as I bled on the grounds before the Beast could bite me again, I wouldn't be so weak for so long. I wouldn't need Arthur's mouth to pull the fever from my body.

When I'd woken that morning, he'd been pacing near the fireplace. As soon as I'd called his name, he'd left and Piffle arrived less than a minute later. But I had questions for him that I planned to get answered.

Piffle brought over a plate of small treats. Cookies iced with a sugary glaze, brambleberries filled with rich chocolate. I bit into one, relishing in the tart of the berry mixed with the decadent chocolate. "My son's wife would love these," I mentioned offhandedly, thinking of some way I could get them to her.

"They're easy enough to make, Mistress. It's finding whole brambleberries this time of year that's the tricky part." He plopped onto the settee next to me, tossing one into his mouth.

"Do you enjoy baking sweets, Piffle?"

"Oh, yes. Cooking for the Master—and now you—has been a great joy in my life. And now that you're here, I'm finding more joy in sewing your garments. That reminds me—" He slid off the settee shouting, "NOTEBOOK!"

A golden bound notebook popped onto the seat cushion with eyes and that distinct mouth. Almost as quickly, a gold feathered quill appeared. The book opened to a page already littered with notes. I turned my head, curious to glance over what was inside.

The quill spun across the page in some of the finest handwriting I'd ever seen with big swoops and swirls.

Piffle-the-Notebook said something muffled into the cushion as he finished.

"What was that?" I questioned, jumping only slightly as he changed back into his fae form.

"I was asking if there was anything you need at the market? I'll go in the next day or two before we're run clean out of food."

I shook my head. "Thank you, but no. I don't plan to stay much longer."

Giving me a cagey look, he settled himself back onto the settee, bringing his cup of tea with him. "I think you'll heal quickly with the broth and perhaps some beef, carrots, and onion stewed in as well. We've got to keep your strength up and replenish what you've lost."

"My, Piffle, you take on so many roles here. I do hope Arthur appreciates you."

"He does! We go all the way back to when he was a boy. The Master is a kind soul, and I did miss him terribly when he left Heartstone to live as the Duke of Riche."

"Duke?" I said in surprise. "Of Riche?"

Piffle nodded into his teacup. "The Kingdom of Heartstone Wood has always had close ties to the Kingdom of Riche. It was a few centuries back, I believe, when the title of land in Riche was given to one of the Kings of Heartstone. Some kind of thank you for a service he had done—I'm not sure of the complete history. But when the Master's father died and Arthur could leave Heartstone Castle, he did, and rarely came back to visit his mother."

"But she stayed? Even though Arthur's father was dead?"

"Yes. She'd made a home in that castle and had no life outside of it."

"She didn't live in the Underrealm with Arthur's father?"

He pursed his lips, busying himself with untangling the

tassels of a pillow. "Marianna never loved André. At first, it seemed likely she could. But then…"

"But then?" I pushed.

"No use in speaking of the past, Mistress, when the present needs us to get you well." He hopped off the settee again, rushing away to pull the sheets off the bed. "I'll have these clean in no time. I'll be back shortly with some dinner. Please stay and rest, Mistress." He carried the linens out the door, shutting it behind him.

I despised sitting still. The only time I ever did was with a decent book, and by the looks of this room, I wouldn't be finding one. Arthur had mentioned a library. Perhaps if I started down the corridors I'd find it. All I needed to do was *want* to find it, as he'd said.

I appreciated the pockets Piffle had sewn into my gown, now full of little bottles of curses, clinking softly as I walked the long glowing corridor. I gave up on my high heeled shoes, choosing to traverse the Underrealm with nothing on my feet but the sheer black stockings Piffle had left for me.

My strength was returning quicker than Piffle or Arthur could understand it would. My Goddess heritage was behind me —eons of Ravenfae power invested in my bones, fueling me to replenish all my parts.

Except those teeth marks.

They remained, small, but visible, partially hidden by the cut of the dress.

Each turn along the halls, lit in orange candlelight, pulled me toward what I wanted, until I found myself at the base of the stairs that led the surface.

I turned around, searching for a library door, finding only the one carved in blackened wood. Shivering in the chill breezing down the stairs, I studied the carvings across the door. Just as intricately carved as the corridors throughout the Underrealm, the door was littered with scenes of fae. Their sharp faces and long pointed ears were unlike any I'd seen before. Groups of them were depicted carving into the walls while others were hauling stones across their backs. Stepping away from the door, I saw it for what it truly was—an ode to the makings of the Underrealm.

These were the faekind who had dedicated centuries to carve out every stone corridor and room in this place, and this door showed how they did it. I pushed down on the lock and pulled on the handle. The door was just as heavy as it looked and as I stepped inside, expecting a library full of books, I was instead met with another set of stairs, these leading down into the dark. I stepped back to grab one of the candles from the sconces in the corridor and began my descent.

The steps dipped in the middle—well worn with use, and along the narrow walls, claw marks were etched across the stone from something wanting to get out or something trying to stay in.

"Hello?" I called, nearing the bottom stair.

Silence answered as I crept through a stone archway. I entered a room already lit by candlelight. It flickered softly over an enormous bed draped in crimson sheets, tucked in perfectly as if the occupant hadn't slept there in some days. A black stone fireplace heated the space and a large chair rested nearby. A few books were scattered around the tables and floors.

Obviously not the library, I assumed the room was Arthur's.

I should have left.

A polite and kind Goddess would have done so, but there are plenty of those and I'd never been interested in joining them.

Curious about the man and Beast who had dragged me into this curse, I traced my fingers over the titles of the books, careful not to disturb them. Books full of romantic poetry, sonnets and letters to lovers. Books of mysteries and one or two adventure stories. Arthur was clearly an avid reader, and as I sat to read

Chorus of the Colliding, a book of poems collected from two lovers over centuries, I understood my captor better.

Arthur was a romantic. A lover of the written word clearly, as his notes in fine penmanship littered the margins of most pages. It was as if I could peer into his thoughts with his markings and underlining segments, scratching out his own notes only to have written something more detailed.

I became lost, reading through each poem, each line that told the story of love between two fae who had found each other young and written words of devotion through every stage of their lives. One poem stopped me, tugging at something within my chest.

In all my forms, I've loved you.
In every new skin I've donned, I've loved you.
Every wake, every mossy morning written in dew, I've loved you.
If the Veil had cursed me, I'd love you.
If time had faulted me, I'd love you.
Within each moment of
Breathing,
Beating,
Sleeping, Eating, Loving, Living,
I've
Loved
You.

My first tear fell, spilling onto the page, smearing the carefully written scrawl of a man turned Beast. One line of the poem was underlined.

If the Veil had cursed me, I'd love you.

In the margin, he'd written,

Can you love the one you've never met?

"You shouldn't be here."

I gasped, slamming the book shut and rising from the chair. Arthur stood in the dark stone archway, his chest bare, breathing heavily, and wet as if he'd just come from the plains of snow.

"Apologies," I said, regaining my composure. "I left, desiring to see the library you spoke of and I was brought here. I assumed the black door led to it."

"It does not."

"Yes, I see that now."

"You should be resting in your room." He walked to the bed, his back to me as he shoved something into the drawer of his bedside table. "Are you...in pain?"

"No." I let the word settle between us. The wound did sting a little as if just to remind me I was in the presence of the one who'd delivered it.

He nodded and turned back to face me. "You must have questions."

"I do."

He gestured wide—an invitation for me to begin as he moved to his wardrobe and slid a cream tunic over his head.

"The door to this room," I began, settling back into the chair. "Are those the fae who built the Underrealm?"

Arthur sat on the edge of his bed, folding his arms across his chest. "This is your question? About a carving on my door and not how my mouth eased your fever?"

A flush rose along my cheeks. "I understand the workings of an antidote. It does not surprise me that the Beast's bite is poison while the man's is the cure. That aligns well with how a curse from the Veil would counter itself."

His brows rose in surprise. "I did not know it would work in that way."

I smirked. "So you put your mouth on me as an experiment?"

It was his turn to blush. "The Beast knew. I asked him what to do when you weren't recovering like you should have."

"You can speak to the Beast?"

He nodded slowly.

"And the Beast is capable of speech?"

"No. I communicate with my mind. He has a grasp of some... particular words."

"Such as?"

He shrugged too casually. "Blood. Hunger...others. Simple things. He knew who you were before you pricked your hand. He said he could smell the 'Bringer' which I assumed was the one who brought him to this land from the Veil."

"Curious..."

Arthur stood, grabbing a blanket across the bed to dry his hair. "You should go. I've just come from the surface and it's after the transition that he becomes the most volatile." He folded back the crimson bedding, ready to slide inside. "You really shouldn't be here."

Pocketing the book of poetry without his notice, I headed for the door. "I shouldn't be here at all," I muttered under my breath.

"Reshina."

I made it to the archway, feeling faint and bracing a hand against the stone to keep myself upright. He took a knife from his bedside drawer, tossing it onto the sheets. The silver metal glinted and the handle shone, carved in bone.

"You have a way out," he said softly. "Take it."

I glared across the room, gathering my skirts and leaving him with a determined, "No."

Each step to the door strained my body, but I managed, focusing on sheer stubbornness as a Ravenfae. I pressed the pads of my fingers into the claw marks leading up to the exit, focusing on each one. When I reached the top, I braced against the wood, catching my breath. I'd pushed myself too far too quickly and the desperate need to get back to my rooms washed over me.

I took one step, then two, taking deep breaths each time. I

leaned against the wall leading up the stairwell out to the surface, allowing the biting chill to breeze over my body.

A darkening sky with soft snowflakes falling in clumps of white opened above me. Without much thought, I took one step up. Then another.

If Arthur was resting from his transition from Beast to man, might I make it across the boundary?

I'd call myself a fool if I didn't try...

I'd call myself a fool when I fell down the stairs and broke my neck.

Five steps.

Six.

Seven.

The cold enveloped me.

Make it to the line of snow, I urged myself, continuing until my stocking feet met the light dust of white, three steps away from the top.

I didn't have it in me to shift, regardless of how much stubborn pride I had as a Goddess and a woman fighting for her freedom.

No.

It was not *this* day I'd escape my prison.

But soon, I told myself.

I leaned against the stone wall, sliding down, watching the starless sky darken and listening to the silence only a night of snowfall can bring. My gown pooled around me in a trail of black and roses sprinkled in soft white snow.

It was beautiful, really.

I wasn't sure I'd ever appreciated the calm fall of ice to the earth. The blanket it lay over everything, quieting the world to sleep like a timeless lullaby.

Resting my head against the stone, I closed my eyes, promising myself the chill would keep me from falling asleep and freezing to death. Minutes passed and my mind wandered back to that place in my dreams—my wings encased in ice. Searing pain, burning, blazing, then a form over me, heavy, a mouth over my skin.

I understood now what it was.

Who it was.

"You're supposed to kill *me*, not yourself."

I jerked my head, eyes flashing towards the voice.

Arthur sat a few steps down on the opposite side with his back against the stone. "I told you to get some rest."

I closed my eyes again, numb to the cold around me. "You cannot tell me what to do, King of Heartstone."

He uttered a foul curse under his breath as he shuffled up the stairs. I couldn't get away from this man. Even if I'd wanted to run, he'd have caught me this night. I was too weak to even try and so, like a child, he lifted me into his arms with the ease of a man who spent his nights as a rabid Beast. He bundled me close to his chest and took me away from the cold. I recognized the dream all over again. His body was so warm, heating mine and melting the snow collected on my gown, now dripping a trail of water along the corridor floors.

I couldn't speak so I remained helpless, the fight in me gone as I wrapped my arms around his neck.

"What? No resistance from the Ravenfae Goddess?" he grumbled. "Pushed yourself past the point of arguing?"

"Tomorrow," I whispered.

His chest rumbled and he pulled me tighter to it. I moaned at the heat and the act of being held as I'd never been in all my centuries.

As the night faded and I gave up keeping awake, I heard Piffle's squeak, a door opening, and the great exhale of a man who read poetry, pulled women into the Underrealm, and melted the stubborn will of a Goddess of the Veil.

CHAPTER 24

Arthur

RESHINA TOOK A WEEK TO RECOVER.

The Beast urged me to her door every night of our transition, and I'd wake to Piffle's teacart squeaking down the corridor each morning. I never went inside her room. Just nodded to the Changlingfae and left.

She didn't leave that week, finally accepting that if she was going to do anything other than collapse, she needed to regain her strength and actually rest.

Anyone else on the brink of death from that bite would have taken a month to recover. But not her.

Not Reshina.

I stood at the entrance of the western corridor, contemplating the days since she'd bled onto my land. As I peered into the dark abyss, a cool breeze brushed my cheeks and the stench of unkempt bodies hit my nose, watering my eyes. I'd been down there twice before.

Once to save Reshina from a sure death.

The other...

The Other.

It was a sure way to die unless a Goddess arrived to save you.

But I could not call what Ishtak did to me a rescue. A curse, maybe. An affliction, most definitely, and the truth of it had been revealed recently. The teeth marks from a Beast remained on Reshina's skin, and therefore, so did I.

She had taken my book. I was sure of it.

I contemplated whether I was irritated at the theft or that she hadn't said a word about it. No snide remarks about my notes in the margins. No questions as to why I'd taken such a liking to poems of love and loss.

Instead, she'd spoken nothing more than simple pleasantries in passing.

Good morning, Arthur. I am well, Arthur. Goodnight, Arthur.

It's all she'd given me and it was all the pleasant remarks I could stand. Worse than silence, I took each one as a hit—a slap to the insignificance I was to her.

But perhaps it was for the best. The longer she saw me as nothing more than a happenstance she'd make her way out of, the more likely she'd kill me one day and take us both out of this curse.

The clack of her thinly heeled shoes echoed in the hall behind me, and I turned instantly, my heart racing at the sight of the Goddess draped in another of Piffle's creations. She wore a tailored black men's jacket, taken in at the waist with a point to the shoulders. Fabric had been added, trailing down her back to the floor while a thin black floral lace made up her skirts in many layers. A long slit split across her left leg, all the way up her thigh.

I swallowed my initial desire, one I was sure she would deny me. "I see Piff is raiding my closet to clothe you now."

Her approach was swift and confident, an eerie power radiating wherever she roamed that sunk into my belly and pulled like a string to her side. I quickly met her across the hall, careful not to touch what the Beast screamed was mine.

"Something you hadn't worn in years, he told me." She

placed her hands firmly on her hips. "Piffle figured you wouldn't miss it."

"How could I, seeing it on you instead?"

Refusing my bait, she lifted her chin. "He mentioned you had something to show me."

"I've barely seen you in a week. Will you tell me how you're feeling?"

Her eyes met the floor briefly. "Fine."

"Fine," I repeated. "You're fine."

Her chin lifted even higher in an impressive attempt to look down at me, though I towered above her. "What is it you wanted to show me?"

I looked her over, deliberately taking my time.

She radiated otherworldly beauty. Anyone with working eyes could see that. But it was the underlying soul of the woman I wanted to get to. To see. To hear. To taste again. I'd known her past for many years of my life, but I wanted to know her *now* as the Goddess dragged into the Underworld, scheming her plans of escape.

"Dine with me," I said, taking another step towards her.

Her head fell back to keep my gaze. "I'm not hungry."

"You are," I laughed. "I hear your stomach churning. I smell your blood working to keep you alert. Your short clipped answers tell me even more so—"

"You cannot possibly hear my stomach or sense my blood. My answers are short because you are wasting my time."

I shook my head. "The Beast can sense these things. Dine with me."

Her eyes shot past me, darting to the western corridor.

"Please," I added, shifting in front of it.

Her hesitation meant the answer was no. But before she could speak, I gave her what she wanted. "After we have eaten, then I will take you."

"Take me?"

"To the library," I clarified.

A deep breath shifted her chest, her jaw sliding across her teeth, and I knew I had her. "One meal."

The corners of my mouth lifted slightly, but I did not vocalize an agreement.

I LED THE WAY THROUGH THE NORTHERN CORRIDORS. The sound of her shoes clicking on the stone kept my heart racing. They granted her another three inches at least, but not quite enough for her chin to reach my shoulders. Why she insisted on wearing them instead of the more practical shoes Piffle had offered, I understood.

Her sleek black heels exuded power.

She made her way through the Underrealm—through life— on little more than air and a sharp heel that announced her arrival wherever she graced herself to be. She'd trekked through feet of snow in those shoes to find her way to my mother's grave and Goddessdamn me if she didn't look good in them.

I knew what Piffle was up to as well with this garb he'd given her to wear. The little man was clever—too clever to not mean to entice me. The Beast was a possessive creature and that jacket, adjusted to fit her, still smelled like me. *She* smelled like me—my sheets, my bedroom—and I was in a rapidly declining mood to be a gentleman.

In fact, I was tired of fighting to present myself as such to her. Arthur, Duke of Riche, knew how a gentleman should behave in and out of the bedroom, but I recognized him less and less since growing into my role as a Beast. Since growing into my role as her captor.

I glanced over my shoulder as we approached the dining hall, looking her up and down again. I could feast. I could feast on her, but I'd have to play my part as long as I could. Regardless of how much I wanted to tear into her, she wasn't a woman to possess. She was a woman to worship. And I would. *Goddess-damn me,* I would until that blade struck my chest.

"Impressive," she murmured, following me into the dining hall.

The corridor opened into another archway detailed in chiseled stone—no door, just a welcoming round room with a long table at its center meant to host dozens of guests.

I pulled a chair for her. "Please." I gestured to the cushion. "Sit."

She did as I asked without a word, instead surveying the table laden with meats and breads and root vegetables swimming in garlic and butter. Piffle had been more than happy to prepare this meal. He'd managed to bring twigs of evergreen woven with red ripened berries from the surface, thankfully omitting the dark roses that grew along my mother's grave.

"I see Piffle has been hard at work," she chided, meaning it as an insult to me.

"He has," I agreed, taking my own seat next to her at the head of the table.

"And what have you done to help prepare this meal? Piffle works harder than any servant I've ever employed." She reached for the plate of venison, spearing a few perfectly sliced strips, still red in the center.

"Chocolat étouffant?" I held the saucière in one hand, offering the glaze to pour over her meat.

Her dark eyes narrowed and her mouth turned down.

I grinned, all teeth. "I've perfected the recipe over the years. The key is the low heat after you've added the chocolate. Also, you mustn't allow it to simmer for too long. The chocolate will become bitter and ruin the richness with the red wine."

She took the decadent sauce from my hand, pouring a heavy

drizzle over her plate. "You've read *Cursed Goddess of the Veil*," she said, just loud enough to hear.

I took my own helping of meat, disregarding anything else. "At least once."

"Tell me then," she said, cutting into her venison. "What else have you learned about me besides my love of chocolate?"

I shrugged. "I am well aware it will take time wearing you down. But I believe you'll get sick enough of this place to kill me to leave it."

She huffed in irritation, taking her first bite. I stilled, waiting for her reaction. It was true. I had spent years perfecting chocolat étouffant, curious about the preferences of the Ravenfae Goddess.

As she chewed, her eyes darted to her plate then back to me. Once she swallowed, she began cutting another bite. "It's perfection, Arthur."

It wasn't the elation I'd expected. My reaction was far too raw for that.

At her praise freely given, I gripped my fork and knife tightly, the whites of my knuckles exposed as I shoved the Beast aside, forcing myself to take a bite and chew slowly. Without even a thank you, I nodded, keeping an eye on her as she continued to eat the meal I ordered Piffle to cook.

The recipe took an immense amount of patience to perfect, and as she cut into another piece of the meat, swirling it around in the decadent sauce, I finally set my own utensils down, fighting with the Beast again.

HUNGER.

"Stop it," I whispered under my breath, clearing my throat and taking a long gulp of wine.

Her eyes darted to me, but she remained silent, finishing her first helping before spearing more with her fork. "Have you spoken to Ishtak as I requested?"

"No. I haven't been able to speak to her."

"But you'll continue to try." It wasn't a question, but I nodded in agreement anyway, lies sitting on my tongue.

"And you'll retrieve me when you do get the chance to speak to her."

Again, not a question, but a command from a Goddess.

My mouth tilted upward. "Yes."

"Good. We're done here. Thank you for the meal, Arthur."

"You've barely eaten."

"I decide that. Now if you could direct me to the li—"

I leaned around the corner of the table, feral with the idea that she was trying to leave my presence. I grabbed a leg of her chair to pull her nearer to me.

In a flash, her long luxurious leg slipped out of the slit in her lace skirts, pressed hard into the stone floor, halting my progress.

"I'm close enough," she chided, rising to her feet when I let go.

"I decide that." I stood, unceremoniously picking up my chair and slamming it down next to hers before grabbing my plate and tossing it in front of me. "Sit down, Goddess."

"I'm not accustomed to being ordered around by a man."

"I'm not accustomed to using this much effort to reign in the Beast, so unless you'd like to have this conversation with him, sit down and eat."

"You're threatening me with the Beast?"

"It's not a threat."

Her eyes followed mine to where black claws quickly grew from my fingers, digging into the table.

She sat calmly, choosing peace for both of our sakes. Picking up her fork again, she stabbed at a roasted carrot, popping it into her mouth.

I took a deep inhale, feeling the Beast's claws retreat back into my hands. Fully human again, I picked up my utensils and continued eating, adding, "You'll dine with me every evening until you decide to end this the right way."

"I—"

"If you refuse," I continued, ignoring what I was sure would be a protest, "I will come to retrieve you. And I will not come as a man."

"Such a gracious host."

"You'll find no grace here, Goddess." I made sure to brush my arm with hers, reaching for another helping. "Only darkness and death."

CHAPTER 25

Reshina

ONCE ARTHUR WAS CONVINCED I'D EATEN UNTIL I WAS full, he swept his chair aside, offering his hand. I took it, accepting his countenance of gentlemanly grace, even though we both knew it to be little more than pretense.

Arthur puzzled me.

In my many centuries, I couldn't recall encountering such a creature as him. The Beast had undoubtedly changed whom I guessed was once a proper gentleman—boring—but proper in his acts and mannerisms. But the man I'd taken great pains to speak little with was like a man at the edge of madness. It was as if he remembered he was supposed to bend to a Goddess, but something inside made him a bit feral instead, causing him to attempt to order me around when truly, he could do no such thing.

Asserting my power was such an effort, and for the time being, I had little desire to fight him when I truly did desire to explore the library of the Underrealm.

When we left the dining hall, Piffle caught us, asking after the meal to which I made sure to praise him exceedingly well, ignoring Arthur all the while.

It didn't seem to irritate him as I hoped, but he smiled at me instead—the corners of his eyes crinkling as someone carefree looked out from them. I admitted then that we must share a true fondness for Piffle and his smiles were honest for the commendation of his only friend.

I walked beside the man down twisting corridors, one after the other, same as the last. "Do you ever tire of such bland halls? Why do you not outfit these corridors to easily tell them apart?"

"I spend little time in them," he answered. "I rarely go anywhere in the Underrealm but my room, the library, or up the staircase."

"I've passed other rooms. What's in them?"

He gave a short shrug. "Dust, I presume."

"Did your mother keep a room down here?"

"She did once. Only because my father forced her. She preferred to live in Heartstone Castle. It's where I was raised."

"Did you come to the Underrealm as a child?"

Silence contained him for so long, I assumed he wouldn't answer. "I wasn't supposed to. But curiosity would get the better of me on occasion."

I looked him over quickly, curious again about his scar. "You rarely saw your father as human, then?"

"I rarely saw him at all. My mother made sure of that."

"I am sorry you lost both of your parents so young, Arthur."

We stopped before two doors meeting in an arched center. "Thank you. I am sorry for the loss of yours as well."

It's a strange thing to meet someone who knows so much about you. *Cursed Goddess of the Veil* was not widely read outside of the Moonstone and Brackish Wood, but there was my captor, knowing well enough that I lost both of my parents at a mere sixteen—the year I became the Ravenfae Goddess and Cursebringer.

"It isn't fair, is it? You know so much about me, but I am at a loss for what your life has been like. Though I can guess at much of it."

He cracked a wide grin. "Please, guess away."

I stood a little taller, my wings flaring at the challenge. "Alright. You were born a Prince of Heartstone Castle, though you did not live the life a typical human prince would. You grew up lonely, your mother and servants the only souls around you, teaching you the manners of a gentleman, but there was always a looming absence in your life."

His brow rose as he listened. "Which was?"

"Your father. You were the direct result of a curse placed upon him when he was a young twenty-two year old king. The curse came from the Veil, delivered by a Goddess who had no choice but to do so, or it would have grown in...severity."

"I've heard of this severity you speak of. Perhaps if you had allowed it to grow, we could have avoided all of this and killed my father outright."

"It is...uncomfortable to refrain from delivering a curse. I've done it only once before with good reason."

He cocked his head, folding his arms. "And what reason was that?"

"It doesn't matter now. All reasons were my own and it is done." I took a step closer to him, looking over his scar. "When you became of age, you left Heartstone to take your role as Duke of Riche, where you remained a proper gentleman by day and an absolute rake by nightfall."

The corner of his mouth twitched.

"Don't deny it."

"I would never."

"You only returned to your mother at Heartstone when your father died. You knew that she was the last thread between you and the curse, so you took care of her, though not with a deep love for her. She was less of a mother and more of a burden in your life. When she grew ill, you grew anxious, knowing what fate would befall you. You did everything you could to keep her alive, not out of love, but out of fear of what you would become. What you saw in your father. A Beast."

He wasn't smiling any longer. Instead he didn't move, waiting for more. "And when did I begin annotating poetry, then?"

A flash of heat bloomed over my cheeks.

"At what point in this decently accurate retelling of my life did I pick up a pen and write in the margins of poetry books, Reshina?"

I locked my jaw, shaking my head slowly.

"I read a book once," he began, rubbing his chin. "I found it after a night of debauchery. Hungover, sore, contemplating how every day and every night of my life blended from one to the other. My father had great sums of money from taxing his people, you see. He was good at that. And when he was human, he was good at getting people to do what he wanted. But he couldn't spend his marks on anything but fine furnishings here and there—a statue of himself and the comforts my mother needed. So I had more marks than I could ever spend, but four of them I spent on a book that could fit into my vest pocket.

"I don't know what led me into that shop or why I was drawn to such a small book, but I bought it, sat on the bench outside in the winter cold and read it cover to cover."

My heart pounded. I'd penned that book so long ago, copies were bound to be made, but I had no way of tracking how many or where they'd gone.

"I left the bench and picked up a chocolate croissant on the way back to my flat. And do you know what I did when I got there?"

I stared, daring him to go on.

He moved closer, my own feet following until I could reach out and touch him if I'd wanted to.

"I read it again. The next morning, I took a walk, replaying the words—the story of a Goddess and what became of her once she'd been cursed at sixteen years of age. I didn't go out that night. Or the next. Instead, I found myself back in that book-shop, asking for more. When the clerk explained there wasn't any, I turned to other books instead."

"You fell in love with the written word."

"I did. But not just any. For the first time in my life, I found purpose in more than just what was expected of me. More than a quick fling or another ball for some duchess or princess. I found that there were books I enjoyed and books I hated. Books I wanted to write my thoughts in and books I flung across the room in disgust or apathy. But that first story. That one, I returned to time and again."

I blushed for the second time, unaccustomed to it and drop-ping my head. "How interesting for you that you should capture the author into your curse."

A hand, smooth and strong, lifted my chin. His voice dropped low, as he shook his head. "Interesting is not the word I would use."

I was never a woman to back away from a man, but I did then. Out of his grasp—out of the reach of his fingers that grazed over my skin, sending chills up my spine. "Well," I started, pulling at the sleeves of my jacket that was once his. "We seem to have a better understanding of each other. May I see what's behind these doors?"

He dropped his hand, turning to them. "The thing about owning a flat in Riche is that they aren't built to hold the collec-tion of a true reader. So, as my mother's health declined and I came to accept the curse that would befall me, I sent my collec-tion here. Where it grew."

He pushed hard on the twin doors. Brilliant light filled the room and I shielded my eyes. I gasped at the sight, for we entered a massive round room with bookshelves rising to the domed ceiling where the shelves curved along the detailed archi-tecture in dark wood. A glass dome above saturated the room with the light of the winter sun. Several ladders lined the walls on golden metal rails. Fine chairs and small couches were placed over woven rugs, giving the circular room a cozy aura. A great black stone fireplace curved between the bookcases opposite the entrance and Arthur headed toward it, adding a few more logs, encouraging the flames to rise higher in the grate.

I stepped forward in awe of the library, having seen many in my lifetime, but none as impressive as this. I squinted in the light, rising on my wings to get a better look at the books lining the ceiling.

Each was nestled into a bookcase with a lip of wood so the books would not fall from the rich walnut cases. On closer inspection, dainty flourishes and fat babies with wings had been carved into the bookcases, often depicted with bows and arrows. I lifted one book, then two, bringing them back down to the main floor, where I sat on an emerald green settee, carefully opening the pages, searching for his marks in them.

"How do you reach the ones on the curved ceiling?" I asked, setting the book aside when I found he had not written inside it.

"When I brought most of these books to Heartstone, I had Piffle place the ones I liked the least up there. He occasionally transforms into a hawk to retrieve them for me."

I set the other two aside, more curious about the books Arthur did enjoy. Beginning at the door to the left of the entrance, I traced my fingers over countless spines of deep burgundies, royal blues, earthen browns, and forest greens. I circled the room, pondering where to even begin when he stepped in front of my path.

"This library is yours as well. You may come whenever you'd like. You may take whichever books you wish back with you to your room. Any others you'd like to add to the collection, you only need to ask Piffle and he shall see to it when he arrives in town weekly."

I took another look around. There were thousands of books on the shelves with more piled on small tables and a desk near the fireplace. "How could I ask for more books than these? I'll never be able to read them all in such a short time."

"Reshina." I met his eyes. "If I were dead, these would all be yours. I have no heir to leave them to. Piffle has no desire for any but a few to remind him of the man he once knew. These books are yours now. I am giving them to you. You need only take my life and you may claim them."

A short laugh escaped me. "Are you bribing me with a curated library in order to kill you?"

"If it works," he said with a beastly grin.

"If you don't mind, I'd like to read instead of spilling your blood all over these fine carpets. Now kindly direct me to your books on the history of faekind."

ARTHUR WAS WELL VERSED IN THE EONS OF THE FAE IN Revelry. The two stacks of books he pulled were just from what he could remember he had off the top of his head, claiming he would need to search through his detailed log of every book in the library and the books he needed to re-shelve from his rooms.

I left the library after an hour, a stack of ten in my arms. Seven on the history of faekind throughout the realm, one specifically detailing the Goddesses of the Veil, and two more books of poetry I'd gathered without his knowledge—taking them from a small table near the library doors.

I declined his offer to escort me back to my rooms, instead requesting he search for more of the books I needed.

It was only when I assured him I did not need his assistance in finding my rooms that I headed to the staircase instead. I thought of those stairs leading to the surface and the possibility of my freedom, and I stumbled upon them quickly enough. I set the books carefully at the base of the stairs, glancing at the black door leading to his rooms.

Up I went with more strength, my body fueled and ready, knowing Arthur was somewhere in those corridors, and I had to take this opportunity.

I left my shoes at the base of the stone staircase, shifted into a raven, and flew out into the bitter cold, my wings pumping me forward as I reached for the edge of the sky, searching for my freedom.

CHAPTER 26

Arthur

IT WASN'T UNTIL THE BEAST WOKE THAT I REGISTERED what Reshina had done.

In declining my help and setting me with a task I found interesting, she had distracted me enough to attempt an escape from the boundaries of Heartstone Castle.

But the Goddess did not yet grasp the will of the Beast.

He roared, transforming before I could stop him and there we were, racing through the corridors once again, leaving deep scars in the stone as we slid around corners with one single purpose.

HUNGER. MINE. OURS.

I didn't attempt to rein him back, my own desires for the Goddess far too developed and my heart buried too far underground to be considered a man with morals any longer. I wanted the Ravenfae Goddess to end me, but not until I'd had a taste, a mouthful, another moan, another sigh, and she ended me in a different way tangled in my bedsheets.

The Beast made it to the surface in record time, focused on the hunt, hardly sniffing the air before bolting forward, leaping over the frozen hedges like an echo of the last time she'd attempted her escape.

Her black feathers reached high above the castle towers. She was flying upwards instead of racing the Beast to the edge of my lands. Clever Goddess. The Beast prowled below her, circling and watching. Waiting for something to happen.

"She'll escape. There's nothing we can do."

WAIT.

My mood turned sour watching her climb. Reshina was leaving me and I'd only just gotten to touch her. To know her. To show her.

WAIT.

"What exactly are we waiting f—"

Reshina fell from the sky in a rush of black feathers, shifting to her Ravenfae form mid-fall and landing in a heap of black lace at the feet of the Beast.

His roar echoed through the gardens and he bared his teeth, encasing her under his form. He nestled into her neck, opening his maw for another bite when the ground shook. She'd beaten him to it, opening her skin and bleeding into the snow before his teeth could sink into her flesh again.

I pulled her to me as we fell and the Beast melted away, leaving the man twisting to take the fall for her into the corridors of the Underrealm.

Rock, dirt, roots—I shielded her from all of it, wrapping my arms and legs around her, never dreading the landing, but already grieving the moment I had no excuse to hold her to my chest.

My back slammed into solid stone, cracking below me. I inhaled sharply through my teeth, still holding onto frozen wings, both of us heaving sharply, adjusting to the warmth and the position we were in.

"I had to try," she panted.

"You were right to," I gritted, pain seeping into my spine as my heart slowed.

She lifted her head from my chest, pulling herself out of my grasp. "I flew up, thinking the Beast couldn't get to me and I'd be able to escape across the land from there. But I couldn't get any higher and then...my power...it just left me. I tried to stun him but that didn't work, either. I managed to shift, but I could no longer fly."

I tested the strength of my back, deciding I'd be left bruised instead of broken. I sat up, running my hands through my hair. "You are confined to this curse. It's unlikely you'll escape through leaving its boundary. The Beast was waiting for you to fall." I shrugged, rising to my feet. "He knew you would."

She met my stare. "I cannot stay, Arthur."

I nodded, starting down the empty corridor. "I know," I said gruffly. "I know."

THAT NIGHT WE DINED TOGETHER. SHE ANSWERED MY questions about what she was searching for in the books she requested. She wanted to know more about the Underfae. When they'd settled in Revelry and where. She wanted to know what they looked like, what habits they possessed. I was well aware I had no such books that could answer her questions. The Underfae had been little more than footnotes in faekind history. The most I'd ever found was that they dwelled in the Under-realm, preferring the dark cold stone to sunlight and fresh air.

But Reshina didn't need to know I couldn't help her. She only needed to know that I was trying. One day she'd grow impatient enough to truly leave. Until then, I'd discover all of her I could. The way she found humor in Piffle's transformations. The way she cut into her food, spearing little more than a nibble, taking all the time in the world to eat just one meal.

I savored those dinners together as they continued. Each day for weeks, I looked forward to them when I woke and mourned them when they ended each night. With Piffle's help, I planned each one, just waiting to hear what she thought of the savory dishes and decadent desserts Piffle excelled in creating.

The Beast roamed the surface less and less each day, relinquishing his hold sooner so I could return to Reshina for our evening meal.

He ate less, complained less, and only looked forward to one thing.

The Hunt.

Everyday for three weeks, Reshina attempted an escape.

Most often when I slept, I'd wake to the Beast tearing through my room and rampaging up the stairs into the freshly fallen snow. Now, she'd tear into her skin well before he caught her, falling into the Underrealm as the Beast leapt after her, leaving me to transform, attempting to break her fall each and every time.

My back was sore muscles and dark bruises, never healing over before more appeared in tandem. I didn't care. I'd take on more, forever, if it meant I could take a moment to breathe in the scent of her skin as we landed. If it meant I had an excuse to sift my fingers through her hair pulled tightly atop her head, but loosened in the fall.

After a month, it was routine. After a month, I resisted asking for more, taking more. After a month, I'd grown into a settling. And settling was a dangerous place to be.

CHAPTER 27

Reshina

THE BEAST WAS UNLIKE ANYTHING I'D EVER BROUGHT beyond the Veil before. When the curse had arrived, I'd placed it in a vial as a dark, twisted thing, same as the others, but power-ful, vibrating against the glass. From the start, it had been far more potent of a curse than what I usually carried to the poor soul who would need to endure it.

And as I hid in the frozen shrubbery not two hundred paces from the staircase leading out of the Underrealm, I took precious few moments to study the creature who, through sheer fate or irony, had trapped its bringer into the curse with it, wholly enjoying the chase and inevitable dripping of blood upon the snow.

The Beast was twice the size of any man, fae or human, with fur so dark, you'd think it black as a starless night unless you were a Ravenfae, prone to see details others could not. His fur matted in places—wavy, sometimes curling atop his massive head with two black horns segmented and sharp protruding from his skull.

I'd caught ahold of them once, attempting to yank his head to the side before he could bite down on my skin, but the creature was powerful, a monster built for one purpose—to hunt, to bite, to feed. I'd narrowly escaped his teeth that time, and I had been much more careful since.

The hunt meant more to this creature than I could have guessed, and though the Beast had not bitten me again, his teeth had scraped over my shoulder the day before, breaking my skin and leaving a tantrum of a wound to show for it.

The sting rose to the surface of my mind as I thought of it, keeping an eye on where the Beast sniffed the ground, his great black eyes searching for his prey.

He'd uncover my scent soon enough and bolt toward me, hidden between the needles of the shrubbery. My sharp nails were poised, ready to cut into my arm until the last moment. I'd questioned to myself many times why I still tried to escape—why I didn't give in and search for another way to leave. The truth of it was, the Beast and Arthur... intrigued me.

A dichotomous being who would show its other side often enough, there were times Arthur proved a sharp tongue and beastly manners at our dinners together. If I ever attempted to leave a little early, he'd remind me not to tempt his strength against the Beast. Then he'd bring his chair right beside mine again, eating next to me in silent restraint.

And then there were times the Beast chased me down, but paused before his teeth dove toward my flesh as if the man inside held the willpower to stop him, giving me the few seconds I needed to rip at my skin and bleed onto the snow.

We found ourselves in a strange limbo, me doing what I could to find a way out of the curse, him reminding me there was a solution I could take.

But I had no immediate plans to kill Arthur. It would be a desperate day indeed for me to take a life from the Realm I was stationed to protect... especially his life.

The Beast caught my scent, rummaging through the snow, his black eyes darting to the line of shrubbery where I pulled my knees close to my chest, my heart racing in a thrill I'd never felt before. His lips curled upon his maw as he stalked toward me on all fours, keeping our gaze locked.

It excited me, the hunt.

At first, I attempted escape purely to do just that.

But somewhere around my twentieth attempt to leave, I found my body atop Arthur's as he broke our fall and something stirred deep within me—something I knew well enough to name.

Lust.

I toiled over offering myself to him as a distraction for both of us while we researched together each evening and dined at the same table each night. I knew well enough that Arthur was curious to better know the woman he'd read about in that Goddessdamned book. Perhaps he saw me as a conquest, a woman to fuck and add to his line of warm bodies in his bed. A Goddess of the Veil would be quite the notch in his bedpost and a Beast the same in mine.

I could do it, I thought, staring down the monster taking his time, prowling over the snow toward me. I could fall through the earth and let my thoughts be known. Would he take my offer? Would he agree to the distraction from the many days here in the same routine we'd established?

Arthur was a handsome man. Built of dense muscle and hands—hands that could bring a fae Goddess to her knees, I was sure of it.

Heat flushed up my cheeks as visions of just what we could do with those hands flashed through my mind. I was not accustomed to such a long spell without a bedfellow, and my body betrayed me there in the frozen maze because I wanted him to catch me. I was looking forward to the fall.

The Beast stopped, sniffing into the chilled wind. A light dusting of snowfall blanked his fur. He turned his head, closing his eyes and I frowned. What was Arthur saying to him in there? I knew he could speak to the Beast, but what could he say that would stop such a powerful creature from what was his nature?

The Beast strained, fighting against himself, a clawed paw stepping forward, then pulling back. Whatever had just happened, the two were at war with each other, the deep, guttural growl of the Beast not meant for me, but someone else.

Without warning, the Beast shot forward, having won whatever argument they'd just fought. With less than a second to spare before my flesh was torn open, I cut my forearm, bleeding, falling, and reaching.

The transformation happened so quickly each time, I struggled to notice the details. We had just begun to fall through the earth when it was Arthur, not the Beast reaching out for me, pulling me to his chest and twisting through the hole in the ground, ready to break our fall once again.

This time, we landed in the kitchens with Piffle crying out in shock and Arthur landing on top of the central countertop, breaking his fall over onions and chopped carrots in preparation for the evening meal.

The landing split the scabbing skin at my shoulder and I hissed through my teeth, sitting up over Arthur to inspect the throbbing cut.

"Mistress! Master!" Piffle cried, rushing to the counter. "Are you hurt?"

I swiped a finger over the wound, bringing a thin trail of blood across my fingertip. "I'll live, Piffle," I muttered, turning my attention back to the man beneath me.

I straddled him, my deep purple skirts bundled up to the tops of my thighs on the sides of his torso. The stretch of my legs over his wide body was the pleasurable type of pain, stinging slightly at the pull. That same heat rushed through my veins and a slow smile lifted my lips as I braced my hands on his chest. "Are you hurt, Arthur?"

His fingers on my waist squeezed tighter and the evidence of just how unhurt he was grew beneath me. "No," he growled, lifting me with ease and setting me solidly on the counter beside him. "I'll see you at dinner."

Stalking away, I called out to him. "If I were to attempt that again, right now, what would happen?"

"Don't," he said without turning, exiting the kitchens entirely.

I huffed, crossing my arms at my chest and leaned against the counter. "That man is such a mystery to me, Piffle. And yet..." I trailed, scraping my hand across the cutting board to gather the chopped carrots back into a bowl.

Piffle joined me, stepping onto a stool to reach across the surface and sweep the diced onions into his hands. "Yet he is simple enough to understand, Mistress. CHOPPING KNIFE!"

I pressed my lips in a grin as he shifted, continuing his mincing of the garlic as he spoke. "The Master desires one thing and one thing alone."

I nodded, biting down on a circle of carrot. "To escape the curse, I know. I cannot help him there, Piffle. And I won't kill him."

Piffle-the-Chopping-Knife continued across another bulb of garlic. "He isn't so bad, Beautiful Goddess. Once you get to know him a little better, you'll find your heart softening enough to say—"

"I cannot say those words, my friend. My curse does not allow me to love."

The little man shifted back into a fae. "Are you sure you cannot?"

"I have been cursed for over five hundred years to never love. I have not said those words since I was sixteen years old."

"Then...truly..." he trailed, gulping loudly, "the only way you can escape..."

I hummed, dusting my hands over the bowl of scraps. "As I

said, I'm not driving a dagger into his heart. There must be another way."

CHAPTER 28

Arthur

BLOOD.

"No."

CONSUME.

"Go to sleep."

DESIRE. WANT. NEED.

"Your vocabulary has increased."

NEED HER.

"Rest."

DESIRE HER.

I slapped a pillow over my face, screaming into the soft down. It was better than the alternative of hunting Reshina down in the corridors and consuming everything between her thighs right then and there, which was exactly what the Beast wanted me to do.

GO GET HER.

"It doesn't work like that," I seethed, tossing the red velvet pillow across the room.

"Hello?" her voice called from the stairs that led into my rooms. "Arthur?"

The Beast gave what sounded like a dark chuckle as Reshina peered around the stone archway. She had pinned her hair back into place, omitting the silver crown she usually wore, replaced with a twig of holly that grew in the hedge maze.

MINE.

Forcing a swallow and the Beast away from the front of my mind, I took a deep breath. I didn't bother covering my bare chest, but slid my hands behind my head on the bed instead—out of reach of her and any sudden moves that might overcome my thoughts. "Have you come to kill me?"

She took my question as an invitation, slipping into the room on her heels—a melody across the stone floor. She wore the same purple gown ruffled at the waist with sleek lines along the bodice and black lace along the neckline.

"No," she said with a grin.

I wiped my hands down my face in exasperation. "Then get out."

"I simply wanted to return this."

I heard the soft thunk of something landing on the bed.

When I sat up, she was already turning to leave. I was desperate to make her stay. "What did you think of it?" I picked up the book of poetry—the one she'd taken from my rooms that night she'd discovered them.

She waved a hand behind her as she turned to go. "You'll see," she called dismissively, her shoes sounding up the stairs quickly before I heard my door close behind her.

I flipped through the pages, curious at what she meant.

She'd added notes.

And her handwriting was...messy.

I laughed out loud to myself, flipping through the pages to discover her quick scrawl along the margins of some of the poems I'd left blank.

The sunlight dapples on frozen sheets.
And still my bed is empty of you.
The frost licks over tall grasses, iron fences,
blanketing every surface.
And still my bed is empty of you.
Must you go, my love?
Must you leave me in the coldest of seasons,
when all hope is lost,
and the loss of you might last a lifetime?
Oh, moonlit night when the stars cannot shine above us,
for the sky weeps in the absence of you—
in frozen tears shed softly
to the soft skin of my cheeks,
where your kiss once lay, I perish with the thought
that you will never return to me.

There in the margin she wrote,

> A bit dramatic, really.

I laughed again, flipping to the next poem I'd never noted.

the ease of my fingers through
your dark curls
begs me to forgive
this endless want
inside me.

Her script tore across the bottom of the page.

> Are these the "dark curls" I think he's referring to?

I knew I loved her then.

One simple jest at a poem written in the language of love sealed any wonderings I'd had on my feelings towards the Ravenfae Goddess of Revelry. Previously infatuated, quickly obsessed, I recognized that something more had grown within me. And until I was dead, I'd be tormented with her presence, never resting, always filled with hunger for her.

With a smile that could not be doused, I laid back and read the notes of the woman who had captured my attention many years ago, and held the entirety of my cold heart in her warm hands.

Reshina

ARTHUR WAS UNWELL.

It was clear by the stiffness in his shoulders—the edge in the way his jaw flexed as he chewed the braised beef Piffle had prepared with red wine and a melody of carrots, onion, and potatoes. He'd developed a tick since I'd seen him last—returning the book of poetry where I had annotated my thoughts alongside his.

He'd changed his clothes as I had mine, and each time I turned to look at him, his eyes would dart away with a sharp turn of his head.

"What bothers you, Arthur?" I asked, daintily slicing into a golden potato.

"You," he answered in a clipped tone.

"Me? I've done nothing to—"

"Your choice of gown, Goddess. It seems Piffle is out for blood."

I glanced down, observing the newest dress. With a silky black bodice and heart shaped neckline, my shoulders were exposed, a tie wrapping around each of my arms and trailing down the gown. The set of teeth marks just below my neck and a red slash along my shoulder were bright red and a decent replacement for any jewelry the gown needed.

"So I must cover myself or sit at dinner with a man who sulks?"

"Wear what you like. But I may sit here sulking in order to control the Beast while you do. Your wound is still fresh. I can smell your blood. I'm doing everything I can to keep him from launching from this seat, Reshina."

"Sorry to disturb your peace, then. Suppose I could take my meal elsewhere." I rose swiftly, egging him on and picking up my plate. I was growing rather fond of this teasing.

"*Sit. Down.*" Arthur enunciated each word while his hands gripped his fork and knife. I admired his hands—the way the veins surfaced across his skin. The way his knuckles shifted from red to white as he bared his teeth in more commands I had no intention of following. "You will finish your meal. Then, you will slowly leave. You will not turn your back. You will not retire in the library. You will go to your rooms and *bar the Goddess-damned door.*"

"Hm," I huffed. "I think not." I set my utensils down on my plate, picked up my glass of wine and took a sip while still standing. "I have a proposition for you, actually. One I think both you and the Beast will thoroughly enjoy."

"Reshina...please..." He met my eyes, his voice pleading.

"Since you seem to be on the edge of ferocity, I'd like to offer something in exchange for my help with a small...project." I set my glass down, slowly, careful in my movements. "I will allow the Beast to bite me again and for you to ease the fever that follows."

He certainly wasn't expecting it. His hands relaxed and he shook his head slightly, dumbfounded for a few precious moments.

"If," I continued, taking a short step away from my chair, "you help me capture an Underfae."

"No." He returned to his meal, head down, slicing into his meat with careless abandon.

I took another step back. "Oh? Surely you and the Beast want what I offer."

"The Underfae cannot be captured."

"I have ideas on that front."

"And I will not risk the Beast's bite on you again. You nearly died."

"And you were there to save me," I appeased, taking another step and adding bluntly, "With your mouth."

Arthur slammed the point of his knife into the table and bolted from his seat, the chair flying out behind him. The knife handle swayed at the force, making a warbled sound between us. He pointed at it. "Take it. Take it and drive it into my chest. Ease me from this madness." His breathing came harsh as he stiffened his arms, his hands lain flat on the surface of the table. He shuddered as he breathed, letting his head fall between his shoulders.

I took another small step towards the arched exit.

His eyes darted in my direction, his face surprisingly stoic. "I am a gentleman," he began.

"You're hardly one of those."

"A Beast, then," he snapped. "Whatever I may be, I am bound to you. And you to me. Whatever notions you have that the Underfae can help you leave—"

"I need their venom." His eyes narrowed but I continued. "Whatever was in their bite, it did not allow me to heal for some time. You retained their marks as well." The distance between us grew as I took one more step away. "If the Beast can be... poisoned for a short while, I will have more time to escape him. I need only thirty more seconds and I can leave the boundary of this land before he can catch me."

Arthur's eyes fell to the floor, his mouth settling into a frown. "You will not kill me, but you will poison me?"

"I do not want you dead, Arthur. I just want you...slow." A shiver ran through me, images of the double entendre dancing through my mind.

"I will do it," he conceded. "I will help you without the bite." He turned back to his chair, lifting it from where it fell on the floor. "Go. We will discuss the details of the plan in the morning."

"You do not wish to bite me?"

"It is unnecessary and risky."

"Tell me, did the Beast settle after he bit me? Was your mind clearer, your ability to hold him at bay stronger?"

"What of it?"

"I'll need your clarity. I'll need *you*. I cannot have you roaming the surface for half the day when it comes time to capture the fae and extract its venom. If that means the Beast must get his taste for my blood to ease from yours, so be it."

"Reshina," he growled, refusing to look at me.

I took several steps back, slipping out of my heeled shoes in the process. "You see my logic and yet you refuse what you want. I'm offering myself to you." I reached the stone archway that led into the corridors. "Take it."

His head turned slowly, eyes black as an obsidian night, replacing the steely blue. The planes of his face hardened, and the corners of his lips lifted as he gave me his answer. "Run."

Arthur

I COUNTED HER FOOTSTEPS DOWN THE CORRIDOR BEFORE I heard her shift—the flap of her wings growing distant.

BLOOD.

"You must control your bite," I spoke through gritted teeth, watching the change come over me. Fur, almost black, grew over my arms as they widened. Claws, sharp as knives, curled over my fingers.

BLOOD. BRINGER. NOW.

"If you truly harm her, I will find a way to impale myself on a sword and end us both."

HUNGER.

My body shifted fully in a torrential rage. The Beast, free of the control I'd held since catching a new scent on her earlier that day, flipped the dining table on its side before he tore through the corridors. Hunting, salivating, fueled with need, I felt it too, deep within the confines of my soul.

Questions of why she'd smelled that way, why the Beast had caught the scent of desire, had plagued me all afternoon, and sitting with her there at that table while she ate and the scent lingered over her skin... It was a divine moment indeed that I had kept myself together. She could have worn a potato sack and the Beast would have roared and raged, recognizing in her the same desire in me.

A Beast could not understand the intricacies of our relationship. For him, blood was blood, hunger was hunger, and sexual desire was easy enough to satisfy when both of us had felt it.

The Beast's claws dragged along the corner of the wall leading to the staircase. Bits of chiseled stone flew across the floor, hitting my door and shattering to dust.

Goddess, he was the worst I'd ever seen. A bellow of the promise that was coming for Reshina shuddered over the stone, shards crumbling from the ceiling as he climbed the stairs, turning all thoughts to the scent of her.

I peered out from his gaze, seeing the world in his black and white and red. It was all he cared for, the hues of red. The blood from a fresh kill, the marks he'd left on her. In a moment of clarity, I regretted allowing her to do this. I should have walked away. I should have let her leave the table.

I'd never been challenged to keep the Beast at bay for this long and with this much difficulty. I'd need to put everything I could into holding him back from ripping into her flesh in a way that could not be repaired. She'd already keep those teethmarks for years, if not centuries, and new ones would appear from this night, but I could control where.

"You cannot bite her neck again. You will not maim her there."

BITE. BLOOD. MINE.

"Her wrist," I ordered. "You may bite the underside of her wrist, so she may easily hide your mark."

The Beast paused in the snow, sniffing heartily. Reshina was playing with him. She could have been there at the top of the staircase, offering herself and getting this over with, but she was not. She hid, just as she had earlier, and the Beast's euphoria flooded through me, heating my blood into nothing more than unsatiated lust.

For there, upon the soft chilled breeze, came hers.

She hid at the side of the castle, under the short bridge leading to the servants' quarters. She hid directly over my rooms in the Underrealm.

"Steady," I commanded as he turned, prowling low over the mounds of snow. "She is offering herself. There's no need to—"

He bolted, flying over the hedged wall and landing on the gravel under the bridge, spraying rocks into the air.

Reshina waited, leaning against the gray stone of the castle, her cheeks flushed red, her chest rising and falling quickly as she caught her breath. "Record timing, Beast. Good. I'm frozen out here already."

It wasn't true. She didn't know she couldn't lie when it came to her temperature in front of the Beast. The blood in her veins glowed a brilliant crimson, hot and succulent, ready to be consumed.

The Beast prowled forward, creeping over the distance with careful strength.

She rolled her shoulders, the scent between her legs permeating the air with a luscious sweetness, her eyes dilated as they flicked over the monster.

"Careful," I reminded him. "Her wrist. Bite her wrist."

The Beast drew a long inhale, his eyes shuddering shut for a moment as he filled his lungs with blood and nectar.

Reshina lifted her chin, turning her face to offer her neck like she had a death wish.

"WRIST," I reminded him, but it was something like my voice that echoed in the dark.

"What?" she gasped. "Did you just speak?"

The Beast shook his head in confusion and I mirrored it.

"WRIST," I repeated to him, but the word came out of his mouth.

Her lips turned down as she lifted her hand in offering.

I'd never spoken through the Beast before.

I'd never heard him say a word or utter more than a monster's roar.

But he'd done it. I'd done it.

He turned her hand, wrapping his long claws over her forearm. The underside of her wrist was pale, but the rapid beating of her heart pumped through her veins, glowing in our eyes.

BITE. BLOOD.

"With ease," I told him calmly. "Please."

His tongue grazed across her skin, tasting the surface, savoring the sweetness. I held the reins as he bit down, allowing him one second, two—it was on the third, I told him that was enough. It was on her sharp inhale of pain that I gave everything I had to restrain him from biting harder, sucking on her broken skin longer.

At our battle, her blood dripped onto the rocks and the ground shuddered, opening wide for a Beast and a Goddess to fall back into the Underrealm.

CHAPTER 31

Reshina

THERE WAS NO COLD.

No frozen winter crystalizing my wings.

No icy feathers melting from the heat of his body over mine.

Only fire.

Only flame.

Only the one who could ease my fever.

Who could tame the rapid pulse and pull such sweet pleasure from the wound at my wrist.

I tossed and turned when he left me.

Frightened, fretting, calling for him to return and calm the scorching blood in my veins once more.

He'd leave and I'd moan.

He'd return and I'd *moan*.

The pain of his loss, the pleasure of his mouth returning to my skin.

I'd not changed in years, but I bloomed beneath him.

A dark flower waiting for the breath that could soothe me, summon me, coax me into opening, and I did not see a way out from this place.

I did not see a way out from under him.

I WOKE IN A BED THAT WAS NOT MINE.

In a realm that was not mine.

Under an arm that was not mine.

The pleasant weight drew a sigh from my lips as I blinked slowly, the color red flooding me. Red drapery around his bed. Red sheets, red tapestries around the room—I didn't dare move. I only took it in.

He'd done it. He'd even somehow spoken it, and though I had new questions for Arthur, the time had come to heal and leave this nest to begin the plan I'd been concocting for two weeks.

I turned my head, careful not to disturb him next to me. He held my left hand in his, his other curled across my waist as he slept. His nose pressed to the underside of my wrist. The heat of his breath brought a numbness to the wound that had mostly healed.

"Arthur," I croaked, remembering the scratch of my throat from the last time we'd done this.

The inhale of his lungs was long and slow as he nestled into my wrist, placing a kiss there that sent tingles through my body. "Yes?"

"I need..." My voice trailed as his lips left my skin and both of my bite marks stung in his absence.

Finding my gaze, he returned with the most delicious of grins, spreading soft kisses along the tendons of my wrist. "What is it you need, Goddess?"

I bit my tongue. *Water*. I needed *water*.

"I need..." My words left me again as his tongue spread over my skin and he closed his eyes in rapture.

My breath exhaled in a shudder, the wound pulsing in pleasure instead of pain. "Arthur," I whispered. If he'd asked me to, I'd have lain with him. If he'd asked me anything, I'd have done it under that trance within his rooms, in his bed, under his mouth.

He lifted me to sitting, wrapping an arm around my back and bringing a cup to my lips. I peered at his face over the rim as I drank—gulping the soothing cool liquid and returning to a place of clarity.

"Will you eat something?" He threaded his hand along my neck, holding the back of my head to steady me as he brought a piece of chocolate to my lips, placing it there for me to lean forward and take.

I kept his stare as I pulled it into my mouth, relishing in the smooth texture melting across my tongue. "Piffle fed me broth last time."

"Can I tell you a secret?"

I nodded, leaning forward for more.

He pressed his cheek to mine, whispering in my ear. "I am not Piffle."

A half-snort left me and he pulled back, grinning so beautifully, my heart leapt at his wide smile, the crinkled lines at his eyes, and the shimmer there in the icy blue. "And here I thought you had stayed to take care of me. Not to sneak me sweets."

His smile softened. "I'll take care of you." He drew me forward, letting my tired bones settle on his chest as he pulled me into his lap. "As long as I live. If you'll let me," he tacked on, rocking us, shifting his strong hands through the tangles in my hair. "If you'll let me," he whispered again, leaving a kiss on the top of my head.

And for a reason I couldn't face, a reason I was not allowed to, I wept silently into the chest of the man who soothed away my fever and fed me chocolate.

MY DAUGHTER WAS MARRIED.

Piffle brought the news that had traveled from the Kingdom of the Citrine Cliffs while he purchased goods at the Heartstone market. She'd done it. And I'd had no motherly part in it. The kindest part of me settled, knowing my son's wife, Seraphine, would have been there to help her choose a dress and give her advice about marriage. Not that I had any to give. I'd never been married, never binding myself to a man and binding him to my curse.

I'd begun writing letters in my mind. Words to explain where I'd been and why I hadn't been there to see her off to her new life. But my words were never good enough. And each time I'd started writing my thoughts onto parchment, I would be crippled with the truth that I could never sign them with love. I could never even imply the word throughout my writings. Morella didn't need me. She had family to love her and a husband who would in time. They all would do fine without me and until I could free myself from this curse, I decided to keep the truth of it away from their worries.

I'd been in bed for two days with Arthur at my side for most of the time to soothe my wound. He left once each day for only a few hours, roaming the perimeter of the castle grounds as the Beast, before returning to me where I'd settle with his mouth on my skin. Piffle had eventually forced me to eat something other than chocolate and by noon on the third day, I was well enough to detail my plans to Arthur.

"Rope, a basket, and a blanket should do. We'll need to keep the Underfae in a dark room, so as not to kill it with light." I tapped the parchment on the desk in the library where I'd written a list of supplies. "We'll need to extract their venom as is done with snakes."

Arthur raised a brow. "And how is venom extracted from snakes?"

"We will coat a cloth in my blood and lay it over a bowl. When the fae bites into the cloth, it will eject venom which we will collect."

"You're very confident about this," he muttered.

"The Beast's bite marks and theirs are similar to a snake's. They must secrete their venom with their teeth, but it must not be as potent as yours."

Arthur ran his tongue over his canines. "And how will we get the venom into my blood?"

"I'll have to cut your skin beforehand. We can't be certain ingesting the venom would do anything to you, but direct contact to your blood should work and slow the Beast."

"You'll cut me?" he questioned, raising a brow and tapping his breastbone.

"Not there," I chided, taking his hand and flipping it over to the underside of his wrist. The tendons along his arm rose and the veins just under the surface of his skin pulsed in a deep blue. "Here," I said softly, tracing a purple vein.

When I tore my gaze from the beauty of his arm, I found him staring, waiting for me to see the heat in his eyes.

Good Goddess, I wanted him. Memories of those long days and nights in his bed, as he held me and brought out the fever in my body, lingered between us.

But I needed to leave this realm. I had my people to look after. I had a son. A daughter. I had a family that grew, and a life somewhere above, I—

"When you leave," he started, bringing me out of my daze, "promise me you will not return."

I swallowed hard. "It's possible I can find a way to—"

He squeezed my hand, bringing my knuckles to his lips. "Ever."

"I'll make no such promise. Now, are you ready to begin?"

CHAPTER 32

Arthur

THE DARK BURROWED THROUGH THE WESTERN CORRIDOR like a disease—an omen and a promise. I refused to allow Reshina to be the one bringing the bait, and though she argued thoroughly about her ability to stun a few of the Underfae like last time, I dug my heels in, reminding her it wasn't enough to stop a horde of them. They were less likely to frenzy with me, for it was her Goddess blood they craved.

Something I knew well.

I took the small vial of her blood from her hand, a shiver running through me at the warmth of it. The Beast awoke, rumbling something about flipping open the cork and downing it all in one go. I shut him away—an easy feat, as he'd been more accommodating than ever since biting into Reshina's wrist.

"Are you ready?" I asked her, rolling my shoulders and cracking my neck to the side.

"Yes," she answered. "Piffle?"

The Changlingfae held his lantern high, chewing obnoxiously on his bottom lip. "Yes, Mistress. Though I do think this entire ploy is unnec—"

"Thank you, Piffle," Reshina interrupted. "We've heard your concerns and made the decision to move forward regardless."

"But if you'd just find a way to say—"

"Enough," I ordered, glancing at Reshina quickly and then back down the tunnel. "Let's begin."

I took one of two lanterns from Piffle and started down the dank corridor. The Underfae nested far from the entrance, unable to risk exposure to any light from the opening. I traveled through the rock, wet and dripping from an underground reservoir of water that spread throughout the Underrealm. A pink slime coated some of the surface and I had to catch my balance twice as I traveled on.

When the dark surrounded me and my lantern was the only beacon in the consuming abyss, I uncorked Reshina's blood. Instantly salivating, I swallowed hard, shaking away the deep desire for just a taste. I added a few drops of the dark liquid to the rocks below me, backing up slowly as I did, leaving a trail for some poor, unsuspecting Underfae to find.

The clicking was distant, but clear as more than one curious creature noticed my presence in their tunnel. When the vial was empty, I inhaled deeply, corking the top and shoving it into my pocket. I blew out the light of the lantern, unspooled the rope at my waist, and waited.

Though my eyes worked better in the dark than my human ones had, I could not see as well as the Beast. But my hearing was infinitely stronger. An Underfae crept nearby, more curious than the others behind it. The fae stopped at the first drops of blood, clicking low before the sound of licking reached my ears. I pressed myself back against the tunnel walls, hoping the creature would come close enough that I wouldn't have to chase it down and carry it out of the tunnel.

As luck would have it, this Underfae was braver than its fellow faekind, its face pressed down into the rocks, tongue darting in and out of its mouth as it lapped up every last drop of Reshina's blood. The fae wore strips of cloth, hunched over, arms splayed wide, clicking softly and biting at the bloody rock with obsession.

And there was our kinship.

I sprang before the trail of blood ended, wrapping the rope around the creature's arms and pressing them to its sides. The fae gnashed its teeth, nicking my hand before I turned its body, tying a rope around its legs, and forcing its shriveled form into a ball. I ran down the tunnel, escaping the incessant clicking and scraping of sharp nails behind me.

"Piffle!" I cried out with the first hint of light.

"Ready, sire!"

I squinted with the sudden torch flame and the fae in my arms hissed in pain. I lowered the creature into the golden basket with a woven mouth, nose, and two large black eyes. Reshina was there and ready, quickly covering the basket with a thick wool blanket.

"That was impeccable timing, Majesty. Shortest you've been down that corridor yet."

I caught my breath, hauling the Piffle-Basket up onto my shoulder. The fae inside quieted, listening or stilling for the sake of survival. "Hopefully it's the last time I need to go in there."

"You're bleeding," Reshina mumbled as we trekked through the vast hall, past the statue of my father and the Underfae carved into the walls.

I adjusted the basket, feeling the weight of the creature inside shift as well. "This one got me with its teeth. But the bait worked perfectly. She went right for your blood and was distracted enough that I grabbed her easily."

"She?"

I nodded. "I believe this one could be female. Others behind her were more cautious, but I needed to run or I'd have to shift into the Beast to fight them off."

We had chosen an empty room near the great hall to keep the fae. Devoid of anything but a few old pieces of furniture covered in sheets, the room was small and cut off from any bright lights. With a single candle lit, I set the Piffle-Basket on the stone floor at the far corner of the room. When I asked him to, Piffle changed back into a fae, leaving the creature huddled on the stone, still covered in the blanket.

"Leave us," Reshina said, staring down at the creature.

Piffle squeaked and I grunted. "You shouldn't be alone with—"

Her head snapped towards me. "I am a Goddess of the Veil, lest you forget." She flicked her gaze to the door before returning to me. "Leave."

Piffle backed out of the room, hands over his mouth, eyes wide in fear.

I stepped towards her. "I can help you."

Her eyes softened. "You have. Now go, Arthur."

Everything in me urged to stay. Damn her orders, this was my Underrealm. But I recognized in her the same woman I'd read about. With her countenance of steel, deep down in the heart of me, I knew she could handle whatever this task required.

"I'll be just outside this door. If you need me."

She resumed her gaze on the creature, watching it shaking under the blanket on the floor. "I will not."

The truth stung as I left.

"Master, what can I do?" Piffle chewed on his lips, wringing his hands together.

I exhaled loudly, rubbing my face and leaning against the wall. "Prepare a feast, Piff. The Ravenfae Goddess readies herself to go home."

CHAPTER 33

Reshina

ARTHUR SHUT THE DOOR BEHIND HIM AND I LOCKED IT. With the single candle as my guide, I slipped off the old sheet covering a small table. There, I had hidden the supplies I'd need for the extraction.

A few clean bottles, a bowl, some fresh bandages, and a towel I'd torn into strips were neatly packed into a roasting tray I'd pilfered from Piffle's kitchen. Keeping an eye on the fae, I gathered a few blankets I'd hidden as well, slipping off my shoes at the door and carrying the warm wool from the Citrine Cliffs to the corner of the room.

"There now," I cooed, "it is just you and I."

The fae didn't move as I placed everything out before me, leaving the candle as far from us as I could to hurt her as little as possible when I pulled the blanket away. I shifted my simple black linen skirts up to my knees to fold my legs underneath me. "I'm going to pull this blanket off you," I murmured, tugging gently, meeting a gnash of teeth when her head was exposed to the light.

Curling into the wall as if she wished to meld into the stone, her fangs were barred, a low click resounding through the room from somewhere in the back of her throat. She bundled herself into the smallest space possible, her hands and legs bound tightly.

I looked her over, searching for any sign that this Underfae was the same faekind as the carvings, paintings, and descriptions I'd uncovered over the past few weeks. Her skin was gray in pallor, stretched tightly over thin bones. Rags covered parts of her body, including her chest, and I agreed with Arthur's observation. This Underfae was likely female.

A small splatter of blood had crusted over her chin and her wild, black eyes darted rapidly around the room before settling on me.

"What has Ishtak done to you?" I whispered, reaching out to trace over one of her disjointed fingers, little more than bone.

She bolted towards me, mouth open wide, fangs positioned to dig into my flesh and tear. I was ready. With a short flick of my wrist, she froze under my power—all of her body stilling except for her eyes. I wanted her to see me, see that I was genuine—a Goddess watching over all the faekind in Revelry above or below the surface.

"You need not be frightened. I need something from you, but you will receive the blood you crave in return." I peered into her mouth. She bore two sets of long twin fangs, each having grown in her attempt to bite me. I busied myself preparing the bowl, cutting the surface of my palm and letting my blood drip onto a clean cloth.

"I've been reading about the Underfae," I started, not knowing if she could understand my words. "You were once great sculptors of stone. You built this place." I sighed, looking up at the dim carvings in the slanted ceiling. Listening to my blood drip, soaking the cloth entirely, I continued. "You dug these tunnels and carved these rooms. Even Piffle doesn't know how far these corridors roam. You told stories through your carvings."

I folded the blood soaked cloth, holding it under her nose.

Though she was stunned, every one of her senses were working and with the fresh scent of my blood, her black eyes pooled with hunger.

Laying the cloth over the clean bowl, I held it up to her poised fangs, pricking them through the fabric. Drops of yellow liquid trickled into the bowl.

"Venom," I confirmed, peeking under the cloth to assess how much was collected. After a few minutes, the venom slowed, but she'd given enough for at least half a vial. Removing the bowl and cloth from her teeth, I poured the liquid into an empty bottle, corking the glass and settling it to clink next to the curses in my pocket.

My hand had already healed in the few minutes since I'd opened the wound, and before I removed the spell over her, I tied another rope to the sconce on the wall and around her waist, ensuring she wasn't going anywhere.

"This is the only chance of escape I have left. Please know that." The spell fell around her and she reared back, a whimpering noise coming from her chest. I dangled the bloody cloth before her, and she snatched it with her tied hands, shoving it into her mouth and sucking repeatedly.

Taking the candle towards the door, I blew it out before unlocking it. "Rest here. I will return for more tomorrow. You will not be harmed. That I promise you."

I opened the door just a fraction and slipped out, careful not to allow much light inside. Arthur sat at the opposite wall, arms draped over his legs bent at the knee. He lifted his head at my appearance, silent and waiting for me to speak.

I slid down the door, meeting him in position, bending my knees and slumping my head back against the wall. "She was not always this way."

"There's no record," he started. "Nothing in the library explains what happened to them."

"Ishtak," I sighed, my wings slumping across my back. "All of this points to her."

Arthur flashed me a guilty look. "I never tried to contact her. I said I would, but the truth is—"

"You cannot reach Ishtak in the western corridor and survive, I know." I pulled the vial of venom from my pocket, shaking its muddy yellow contents. "Too much of this and you'd be dead. Yes, light hurts them, but they are so many in number, they would overcome you and your source, snuffing it out and draining you dry. I do not ask you to seek Ishtak for my sake. I do not ask anything of you but to help me leave this place."

"There is nothing else you'll ask of me?" His words cut sharp in the air between us. Memories of the last few days, locked in an endless need of his mouth across my skin, settled like a portrait, flashing in glimpses of crimson sheets and warm breath along my wrist.

He waited for me to say it, waited for me to admit my want for his body, heavy over mine.

I did question it—what it might be like to take my pleasure from him in the very little time we had left before I'd poison the Beast and beat him to the ends of the castle boundary once and for all. The longing was there in his eyes, as he stared at me across the corridor. And I saw the softness in him—the counterpart to the raging Beast within his soul, longing only for the blood of the bite.

"Arthur," I started, but he rose to his feet, shaking his head.

He held his hand out to me, helping me rise to my bare feet. "Never mind." He kissed my hand, squeezing it gently. "Come. Piffle has put together a small meal in my rooms. Something to fill our bellies before we rest."

"Your rooms? My fever is gone. I will return to—"

"If you need to keep the Beast at bay, I suggest you continue sleeping there until...the escape. He is calmer when you are there. He does not rage to be released." He didn't let go of my hand as we walked down the corridor, taking a right at the open passage. "I can sleep on the chaise if you'd like."

"You are warm," I said, squeezing his hand back. "And I am cold. Let us leave it at that."

He nodded, giving me a simple smile and led the way to the black door across from the staircase that would lead me home.

FOR THREE DAYS I CAREFULLY COLLECTED THE Underfae's venom. She had less to give after the first extraction, and though I fed her my blood each time, her feral nature continued—slashing and biting through the air every time I met her in the abandoned room.

The Beast was calm, only roaming a few hours each night while I slept in Arthur's bed. He'd slip back in and I'd turn, feigning fitful sleep to reach for him. I was awake the entire time he was gone, and though I never said it, I yearned for the heat of his body next to mine. We'd wake tangled together, my head resting on his chest, his arms wrapped around me. We'd become two people forced together, but choosing each other's company anyway.

Damn this curse.

Damn the both of them.

In the early morning of the fourth day, I lifted my head, resting my chin on his chest, watching him sleep. Arthur had become a friend in the six weeks I'd known him, and I didn't want that to be the end of us... or what we could be together.

Tonight, we planned for my escape from the curse and thoughts tempted me. Dark ones, salacious ones, soft ones. I would bet all the marks in the Brackish Wood that this man could see to them all, but time was not meant to be manipulated in the lives of those cursed by the Veil.

We had either too much.

Or too little.

And as I stroked Arthur's brow in a light caress, some part of me begged to stay. In all my six centuries of life, I'd spent little of them living for what I wanted.

My children, my people, my title, my crown—all had come first, leaving me a flame doused in the liquid chill of power that came with a price when it was thrust upon me at such a young age.

I had a list of moments where I wished I had the power to stop time from turning. I brushed a finger over Arthur's soft mouth, adding this one to it.

His lips parted as he stirred, and I pulled myself closer, easing my mouth softly over his, brushing over his lips in a ghost of a kiss. His eyes fluttered open, blinking in soft confusion that spun to realization. Sinking his fingers through my hair, he pulled me to him, our mouths meeting in something desperate, something hungry.

He sat up, taking me with him, pulling me into his lap without breaking our kiss, and that lighted spark within me flared, shimmered—proved itself capable of climbing to flame with the caress of him to fuel it.

My hands dug through his hair, which had grown longer in the weeks since I'd arrived. My body raked against his lap, building in pressure for what I wanted—what both of us needed from each other that we'd denied ourselves in this curse.

The most beautiful pair of hands gripped my thighs, roaming to my backside while pulling me in. I met my turning point, deciding then which direction to go.

"I'm leaving you tonight," I whispered between our lips. "If I do not go now, I fear the excuses I'll make to stay."

He pulled away, sweeping his hands along my neck to cup my face. "I understand. They need you more than I do."

I peered into his steel blue eyes, knowing his response for the lie it was. I covered his hands with my own. "One more extraction and we'll have enough."

His lips met mine again, soft and wanting. "Go," he whispered. "Before I beg you for more."

On a sharp inhale, I kissed him again, pulling myself out of his grasp and from his lap. I pulled on my silk robe and left his rooms, refusing to look back.

I'd see him tonight.

We'd planned everything with Piffle.

And as I passed the staircase leading to the lands of winter, I did look back, knowing I'd see him at his doorway, watching the Goddess he'd been infatuated with for years plan her final escape from his grasp.

Arthur

"I LOOK FOOLISH," I GRUMBLED, ADJUSTING THE COLLAR of my jacket. Black beads shimmered through the lapel in an ensemble Piff had shoved me into after a long bath that did nothing to quell my unease.

My stomach crawled up my throat, my heart shredding with each passing minute, well aware of what waited for me this night.

Where once I'd been a miserable soul, living each day like the last for thirteen years, now my future held nothing but gray days and memories of *her*. Where once Reshina had been a distant light, something to hope upon and never grasp, merely written on a page, I now knew her lips, her smile, her way of weaving her authority and power into her words, never demanding much, knowing she'd always get it, so why bother?

Now, I knew what it was to fall.

And right at the point of this realization, she'd be leaving me. For good.

"Master, not like that!" Piffle grew two sizes too large, towering over me and ducking his head to miss the ceiling. Enormous hands adjusted my cravat, fixing whatever mess I'd done to it in nerves and heartbreak.

He shrank back down to his usual size with a satisfied grin on his face.

"That was excessive," I grumbled, checking in the mirror at his work.

"I've been practicing that one," he said with pride, darting around my rooms, picking up books and stacking them on tables. "How else will I reach the edge where the ceiling meets the walls in the corridors to hang the tapestries?"

"Tapestries?"

He nodded, picking up the black leather shoes he'd found for me to wear for the evening. "Mistress requested them. Said they'd bring color to the halls while she is away." He looked up at me with a raised brow. "Said they'd remind you not to lose hope."

"You know she's leaving, Piff."

"Yes."

"And she's not coming back."

With a slight shrug, he continued his work, placing the shoes down beside the bed where I slipped them on. "Dinner is about to be served. I must excuse myself. Is there anything else I can do for you?"

"No. Thank you for watching over me, Piff. But most importantly, for watching over her."

He made an aggravated grunt before I heard a thunk. "Perk up!" The words came from a little golden clock set on the table by the fire, its pendulum swinging back and forth dramatically.

I frowned in deep annoyance, ignoring his antics and adjusting my cuffs.

The clock didn't stop there, however. "You've pined after this Goddess for so long, and yet you let her poison you and leave?"

"I'm not forcing her to stay here."

"Then stop moping about it and spend your last minutes with her!" He pointed to his own clock face. "Look at the time, man! She's there in the dining hall already, waiting for you, and yet you are here, fretting over your collar! If it is she who you want, let it be known!"

I stood in a heavy sigh. "I can't tell her what she means to me. I won't be the cause of any guilt she might feel in leaving."

"*By the Goddess*, Arthur, you are a martyr of your own making, through and through! First with your mother, then with that business in Havenshire, now this! Do not let her go without telling her why she should stay!"

I left the bedside, shaking my head at a clock telling me what I should and shouldn't do. "One last time I'll sacrifice my needs." I swept through the room and headed up the stairs, listening to my one friend scramble behind me. "One last time I'll sacrifice them for her."

I STOOD IN THE ARCHWAY OF THE DINING ROOM, READY to sink into the stonework. Reshina busied herself around the table, her back to me with glorious black wings tipped in silver. She wore one of my favorite gowns so far with long black layers in the skirt that pooled at her heeled feet. A beaded cape of sorts hung at her shoulders, detailed with intricate patterns on each of her arms and shimmering black beads hanging from one shoulder to the other across her back. I understood my own attire now, a compliment to what Piffle had sewn for her.

Her long black hair was pinned at the top of her head, the silvery branches of her crown catching in the candlelight. She was adjusting our plates, I finally realized, taking the silverware from my setting and adding them to the space next to hers. She finished with my glass before turning to pick up my chair.

"Arthur!" she cried, facing me with a blooming flush to her cheeks.

I was wrong. This gown *was* my favorite.

The black bodice curved to her figure, shaped over her breasts with an ample ode to the voluptuous nature of them. The beading at her shoulders hung around her neck, leaving free the small pinpricks of teethmarks at her collar bone.

"You are stunning," I praised, leaving the archway to take her hand and bring her knuckles to my lips.

"Thank you. I see Piffle has dabbled in matching att—"

She gasped as I turned her wrist, placing a light kiss at the bite marks along the underside. Instant heat filled the room, present in my stare, in the way her chest began to heave and her skin flushed red.

TAKE HER.

I agreed with the Beast's demand, but managed to remove my mouth, pulling her chair out for her instead.

As soon as we were seated side-by-side, the telling squeak of Piffle's cart sounded in the hall behind us. He wheeled it in, practically giggling in delight.

"Dinner is served, Your Majesties." Removing the domed lid over a large platter, he revealed a single pie, steaming through the long ovals cut into the crust. He lifted the platter, squeezing in between our chairs with hardly an *excuse me* and settled it between our plates.

"This is certainly unusual," Reshina laughed, sniffing over the golden crust.

"Piffle," I said in a humorous tone, "what are you up to?"

"Why, I've prepared your dinner, sire! You'll not be needing these," he said, swiping the knives from our settings. "Nor these," he added, taking our plates.

"And how are we meant to eat this...pie?" I asked.

Picking up our forks, he took each of our hands, setting the silverware in them before closing our fingers around the silver stems. "With these of course! Oh! And one more thing." He jumped at the same time he yelled, "DECANTER!" shifting into a golden glass pitcher full of red wine.

I eyed Reshina as he filled our cups. She bit down on her lips, desperately holding in a laugh that was on the verge of shaking her entire body as it built. I closed my eyes and shook my head. "Thank you, Piff. We'll meet you in the library when we're finished here."

With a short pop, he bowed at the waist, wheeling his cart as he backed out of the room.

Reshina's laughter burst from her lips as soon as he was out of earshot. I joined her, shaking my head. "I should have guessed he'd do something like this."

She poked at the flaky crust. "What *is* he doing exactly?"

I sighed longingly, looking her over as she bent her head, inhaling the steam. "He's forcing us to eat this together. To get us closer. In a more...intimate dinner."

Her head snapped up with clarity. "You mean we take bites out of this together?" She glanced down at the table. "With nothing to cut into it and no plates to serve it on?"

I clinked the tines of my fork against hers. "No plates, no knives. Just two people sharing a meal the closest we can."

She took her glass, raising it in the air. "To Piffle."

I clinked her glass with mine. "To Piffle, and to the cleverness of the Changlingfae." We took our drinks and dug into the meat pie between us.

CHAPTER 35

Reshina

ARTHUR HELD MY HAND THROUGH THE LONG CORRIDORS leading to the library. I pointed out the two tapestries I'd uncovered in the room where we'd kept the Underfae before setting her free back down the western corridor. I noted that with Piffle's hard work carefully cleaning the fibers, the colors brought a vibrance and warmth to the halls.

He nodded, squeezing my hand as I made him stop at each one, pointing out the patterns and design I thought he'd appreciate.

"If you look here," I said, pulling him closer. "You'll see that words have been woven into this one. It's a language I don't recognize, but I expect you to have discovered it by my return."

He bent forward, squinting and brushing his fingers over dark fibers. "It's Céaduah. The language of the Changlingfae, uncommon outside of the Citrine Cliffs."

I sighed inwardly, having expected it to take him longer to figure it out. I had planned a few tasks for him while I was away—some I left as secret notes in the books he'd read. Some I had told only to Piffle to spring upon him when he seemed at the edge of despair. I was well aware the language was Céaduah. Just as I was aware that I was second guessing this plan to the fullest degree. The words were on my tongue to seek another way to reach Ishtak for help when the pull of violin strings sounded ahead.

"What is that?" I whispered.

"I think you mean *who*."

We followed the music to the library doors, propped open with a golden violin hovering mid-air. Two black eyes and a wide smile bloomed at the base of the instrument.

Arthur pulled me into the middle of the room. The couches and chairs had been moved aside, creating a wide open floor.

"Dance with me?" he whispered in my ear, pulling on the dip of my back, taking my right hand into his left.

Every inch of me screamed to stay. To pull his mouth to mine, to give into this threaded desire between us. Arthur was the want I'd denied myself time and again throughout my life. He represented everything I shoved away, choosing duty and title before anything else.

Stay, my fingers urged, threading through his.

Stay, my lungs breathed as he pulled my chest closer.

Stay, my feet begged as we spun in slow circles to the timing of the music.

The venom in my pocket hung heavily with the weight of what I felt I must do and how easy it would be to toss it in the fire instead.

I swallowed my guilt. "Arthur, I—"

His mouth slid over the marks on my neck, and I turned my head in blissful pleasure, saying goodbye to what could have been.

But I would return to this castle and save its king. That I could promise myself. That could keep me from tossing the vial of venom into the fire.

His mouth traveled up my neck, leaving soft, scraping teeth. I pulled back to see him fighting with the Beast. His hands were claws around mine. His face edged toward something animal—a monstrous creature I'd grown fond of.

"He's fighting you," I whispered.

"He's aware of what we're about to do. I can hold him. But I need you to begin."

I nodded solemnly. Taking the small dagger from his claws, I cut deeply along his forearm. He didn't even flinch at the wound, refusing to look away as I pulled the full vial of venom from my pocket.

I heard the shift from Piffle, standing at the ready to help Arthur eventually recover from the poison. I uncorked the vial, determined not to shake, hovering the contents over the blood seeping from his wound.

He lifted my chin with a claw. "Do not return. Leave me behind forever, but do not go without leaving me something sweet upon my lips."

Before I could choose the path I wanted, I lifted to my toes, kissing him hard and emptying the contents of the vial across the open skin of the King of Heartstone Castle.

The Beast

OUT. LET ME OUT.

"Can't...not yet..."

BRINGER. LEAVING.

"Not leaving...stay a little longer."

LIAR.

PAIN.

HURT.

"It's for the b-best."

HUNT. MOVE.

...

OUT.

BLOOD.

PAIN. DESIRE. WANT.

...

HURT.

GET HER. BRING HER BACK.

...MINE.

Reshina

THE BRUTAL WIND WHIPPED AT MY CHEEKS IN A FLURRY of ice in the winter storm, leaving them raw and red. I couldn't fly, not in this blizzard, so I ran through mounds of snow, using my wings to help guide me forward, away from the man I'd just poisoned.

I questioned my sanity.

I questioned every choice I'd made up to that moment, but the line of the wrought iron fence surrounding the lands of Heartstone Castle loomed ahead, and I marked the end of the hedge maze as the farthest I'd ever gotten away from the Beast.

Had I killed him? Was the venom too much? I turned my head to the yellow glow of the entrance into the Underrealm below.

Or was the poison too little?

A dark figure loomed there, taking up all the space and blocking most of the light. I trekked on, one step after the other.

I owed it to Arthur to leave. To see through to my plans. He begged me to never return, but I would not give up on him. I could never leave him there. My body, even then in the dead of a winter storm, heated at the thought of his mouth on my skin, and I'd get it again.

Goddessdamn us both, I would.

A howl, prickled with an animalistic moan, pierced the air, dampened in the rage of the wind, confirming the Beast had made it to the surface. Arthur was not dead, but by the sound of it, certainly not the same powerful Beast that had hunted me down time and time again.

The iron fence was there—just a few dozen yards. I would make it. I glanced behind me again, a short cry leaving my lips as the great Beast took one more step and collapsed into the snow.

I couldn't stop now. I had to put my trust in Piffle—in Arthur —that he would survive and I would escape. Turning away and pushing aside my fear, I saw the truth of the land outside of Heartstone Castle. The fields beyond the gate were bare—wet and muddy—more proof that Heartstone itself had been embedded into the curse as it grew and grew with each passing year it was not broken. The storm raged only within the castle grounds, and if I could just reach the black gate with its sharp posts pointing to the sky, I could shift outside of the storm and return to the Brackish Wood. There, I'd find help. Through my people, I'd find a way to release Arthur from the binds of his curse.

A long howl sounded behind me again, pained and mournful. I gritted my teeth and dove to the fence, gripping the bars and yanking on the latch at the arched gate. In a silent reply, it did not budge. It did not comply with the force of my grip, so I searched for a lock, a device refusing my attempt to escape. There was none, and the harder I yanked on the cold iron, the more my heart gave way to panic.

I unfurled my wings, flapping into the night, fighting against the wind and hovering to the height of the iron bars to fly over the top to the other side.

I met an invisible wall. Banging against it with my fists, I screamed into the moans of the wind.

It's grown too powerful, I told myself.

I cannot escape the curse by the lands alone.

I tried again and again, using the posts to hoist myself, hovering over the fence, but no amount of force could break through.

I fell back down to the snow, turning at once.

Fear of being trapped forever gripped me, but I shoved it aside, running toward my captor with the cry of his name on my lips. "Arthur!" I screamed, fighting through the snow to the mass of dark fur.

I cried his name again, but the Beast did not stir at the sound.

Through frozen limbs, I reached him. A blanket of snow dusted over his dark form. "Arthur?" I pleaded, pushing at his side, flipping him over to see the Beast, eyes closed, and still. "Please! Hear me!" I cupped the side of the Beast's head, turning him to face me. "I cannot leave!" I grabbed hold of his fur in my fists, shaking him. "Do you hear me! The curse will not let me leave this land!"

Met with growing silence, I sliced a sharp nail along my wrist, careful not to bleed onto the snow just yet. I held the open wound over the Beast, pulling on his jaws to open his mouth and let my blood spill into the night.

His head jerked to the side, before his tongue slipped from his mouth. I laughed in relief. A clawed hand reached for my arm, pulling it closer where he licked thoroughly over the small cut. I yanked my arm away, not willing to risk his bite. His claws ripped at my gown, desperate for more.

The ground rumbled when I wiped my blood across the snow. I held onto the Beast as we began to fall through earth and stone. We landed with a thud, and by the time I lifted my head from his bare chest, the man had returned.

Or most of him.

The arms of the Beast wrapped around me, pressing me to his body. We'd landed in my rooms, on my chaise by my fireplace, lit for us as if Piffle had known we'd end up here all along.

Arthur blinked in a blur, groggy and stunned.

"I made it to the gate, but I cannot leave," I whispered. "The boundary of your land is the boundary of the curse. It will not let me go."

"Is this a dream?" he rasped, squinting hard, as if trying to wake himself.

I leaned into him, sliding my hand along his cheek. "No, it is not. I cannot leave you, Arthur."

"It is a dream, then," he whispered.

"*Arthur,*" I started, but he ended my words when his mouth crashed into mine.

CHAPTER 38

Arthur

SHE DIDN'T LEAVE ME.

And she never would.

The Beast roared in my veins, demanding I tear at her skin with my teeth and do what he could not.

Instead of ignoring him or pushing him aside, I allowed him space. I allowed him to witness what I would do to the Ravenfae Goddess of the Veil. What I would consume that night with this woman within my thrall.

Her gown was shredded in seconds, a beautiful adornment to her body, but very much in the way of my hands on her skin, my tongue on her breasts, pulling the taut peak of her nipples into my mouth, one after the other.

She moaned my name and we were gone from the chaise. I picked her up, ready to tear away her undergarments, finding she wore none.

"Tell me to stop," I offered, pulling at the last strips of black silk tangled between her legs. She laid bare on her bed in sheets of silky evergreen, her wings splayed wide behind her as her skin flushed under the hunger in my gaze.

No gown Piffle would ever create could compare to this. I shuddered, admiring all the inches of her skin—the heavy curves of her lower breasts, the white marks of skin stretched across her hips and belly—the same dark curls she'd laughed about in a book of poems, my epiphany from the Veil to love her for all time.

MINE. OURS. TASTE.

I nodded in agreement, bending over her on the bed, waiting so patiently for her to tell me if she wanted this, too.

BITE. BLOOD. HUNGER.

She reached up, sliding her hands around the back of my neck. "Tonight, I am yours. Consume me, Arthur."

It was all I needed to hear before my mouth was on her again, my tongue exploring hers, my hands returned from Beast, sweeping over her breasts to her back, pulling her to me. Her legs wrapped around me, and I tore free of her arms, sliding my mouth down the length of her body.

A taste. Just a taste and I'd be a better man in the morning. Just a taste of what she'd been giving me between her legs, and I'd be cured of all my greed, my thoughts of elation that she could not just leave me. My sick pleasure knowing that through the fire of her fever, only my mouth could soothe her.

I grasped the underside of her thighs, pushing them back to her torso, sliding my tongue up her center, inhaling in the raw scent and sweetness of her.

An adorable squeak came from her lips, and I smiled with another pass, knowing far too well what other sounds I'd pull from her chest by the time I was through. I took my time there between her legs, holding her underneath me, refusing to ease up even when her nails dug into the back of my hands so hard, I felt the skin break and her body shudder, shaking through her cries of pleasure.

When I was sure she'd had her first release of the night, I slowly freed her legs, letting them fall back down as I settled between them.

Shame on me for thinking a Goddess could be spent so easily.

Her mouth was over mine in seconds, exploring the taste she'd left there, her hands pulling at the waist of my pants, ripping them away until she found her grip around my cock, so hard I thought I'd burst at the slightest of her touch.

She read me like a book, stroking fast, pulling me into a place of such want and need, I could have spilled into her hands right there.

"Take me," she whispered on my mouth. "I must have you inside me."

I became so feral with need, I nipped at her bottom lip, drawing the slightest bead of blood. Instead of shock or anger, she responded in a soft moan, delivering my death sentence, for I would cease to live if she ever found a way to leave me.

I pulled her body to mine, slipping inside her with the ease of a man who knows a woman and the decadent mess he'd left there at the pleasure of his tongue. Within seconds of harsh thrusts, I spilled into her fully, refusing her any room to breathe because my fingers came next, sliding into her, curling against her inner walls, driving a maddening moan from both of us. She reached down and pulled them out, her tongue licking and sucking as if she was starved of the taste of both of us for all of her centuries.

It was enough.

Like a rabid dog, I flipped her, my cock still hard as I pounded into her from behind, gripping her wings and forcing her back to my chest. I bit at the skin of her neck, bringing a cry of pleasure and pain from her lips.

I'd mark her. I'd imbue myself into every inch of her skin so that one day when she did leave, because I was dead, the scent of Beast would follow. Any man, fae or mortal, who touched her would know I'd been there. I was the one who fucked her sense-less. I loved her beyond the limits of skin and bone and sinew. I loved her *everlasting, ferally, completely*, and that would be my legacy.

Not Heartstone Castle

Not the Underrealm.

Her.

The Ravenfae Goddess of the Veil was once consumed by a monster. She would not survive unscathed, but scarred, forever roaming the realm with a Beast upon her soul.

CHAPTER 39

Reshina

ARTHUR FUCKED ME UNTIL I COULDN'T STAND. MY LEGS shook and still he took me again, laughing with me when I fell to the floor, slipping inside me anyway because I begged him to.

As if he was marking me, he came inside me again and again, each time more wild than the last. Each one of my releases was the one I thought would kill me, pulsing around his cock so hard, my body wouldn't let go of him, even as I lay there shaking, crying out for more of his hands, his palms, his fingertips pressing into my skin.

We fucked in the corridors.

We fucked on the dining hall table, a shocked Piffle squeaking and running the other way whenever he happened upon us.

We fucked on the stairs leading to the surface, in his bed, in mine, on the floor in the library in front of the fire.

Days passed into weeks, and I knew only the feel of him between my legs. Only the length of his tongue following the length of my body in an obsession now coursing through us both. When we remembered to nourish our spent bodies, I refused to let him eat with his own hands, giving him every bite, kissing him soundly when I decided he was done—when his rest from me had been long enough.

He claimed me over every surface, and though I saw the feral Beast in him many times, he did not let him out, keeping me over or underneath him from morning to night.

By the time he fucked me against the doors to the library, I'd marked him too. By then, my own teeth marred the skin of his neck and though he healed almost as quickly as me, I was sure to keep leaving the bruises from my mouth along his skin.

I squeezed my eyes shut, gripping his back as he thrust into me so hard against the doors, I saw stars. I wanted to cry. I wanted to scream and tear through the world because finally, I had been given no other choice than to take what I wanted. We had nowhere to go. Nowhere to be. We had each other. We had long, luxurious days of oral pleasure and fast, wild nights of two lovers, two creatures, without limits.

Two weeks into our craze, he surfaced to let the Beast roam. I followed, refusing to let him leave me. The Beast chased me down, relinquishing to Arthur, half Beast, half man as we fell through the earth, my skirts pulled high around my waist, freeing his cock through rock and dirt before we'd even hit the stone floors of the Underrealm.

I rode him the moment we hit, raking my nails down his chest, laughing at where we'd landed. There, before the carved stone statue of his father, I fucked him loud and hard, with the sheer abandonment of every reason not to, choosing Arthur. Choosing myself.

He lifted my hips, pounding into me, the pads of his fingertips digging into my skin hard enough to leave bruises. I tilted my head back and laughed, relishing in the mix of the pleasure and the pain. I screamed his name as I came, him following quickly after. Slumped over his chest, I panted, kissing my way up his neck and to his lips where he joined me in mirth.

"What would your father say?" I giggled.

He turned his head, eyeing the great statue of the hall. "He'd be angry it was you I chose to bring into this curse."

"Chose?" I slid to the side of him, wrapped in his arms. "Your Majesty, I found my own way into this mess."

"Mmm," he hummed, sliding his fingers through my hair and bringing my mouth to his. "What mess is this?" He maneuvered his body over mine, slipping one of his glorious hands between my thighs, stroking his fingers up my center before ending in a slap. I squealed at the sharp bite of pleasure and sting of pain. "Do you think you can manage to be any louder? Let my father hear you in his grave. Let him suffer beyond the Veil, knowing I fucked the Ravenfae Goddess under his monument to himself."

As it was, I could be louder.

Three times through.

CHAPTER 40

Arthur

OUR FEROCITY SLOWED EVENTUALLY.

Four months since she'd bled onto my lands, I fucked her once a day. Perhaps twice. Three times if the sun rose in the morning and set in the evening, and though the Beast still needed to roam the surface, Reshina always followed.

It was a game we played, the Beast more than willing of a participant.

I'd release him on the surface and he'd roam the perimeter of the lands, refusing to hunt deer or small animals, instead always searching for her.

She'd hide somewhere and he'd find her, lunging, desperate for the puncture of his teeth through her skin again. But she always escaped through the ground opening to carry us back into the Underrealm once again.

Except the time she didn't.

It was my fault. I took the full blame. I had become too accustomed to needing the events after our fall. I looked forward to them too much to notice that she tripped over a broken statue in the courtyard gardens, and had not bled over the snow, diving into the Underrealm. The Beast caught on before I did, ravaging her skirts, shredding them before his bite locked into the skin of her thigh, pulling a scream from her lips and a desperate cry from mine.

After I carried her to our rooms, I relieved her of the fever as I had before, apologizing again and again. When my mouth was over her wound, she begged in her fevered state for me to take her. For me to fuck her as she dreamt of me.

I refused.

I pressed my lips over her skin, licking the marks of teeth and she moaned. "*Please*. Please, Arthur."

Goddess, I was so hard, I had to adjust myself. "Not until you can tell me what you took in payment for the cost of your curse when you were sixteen years old."

My tongue swept over her again, and I breathed fully at the heat pooling between her legs. "It was...it..." Her voice faltered as she drifted. She wasn't even lucid enough to remember, and I'd not have her unless all of her was with me.

On the third day, I woke in our bed to her soft lips on my chin, my cheek, lightly pressing over my eyes.

"A rose," she whispered. "It was a rose I wanted the day my life changed forever."

She dropped her head to my chest, her mess of black hair tangled and frizzy. I smoothed it from her face. "Tell me what happened."

"You know this story already."

I lifted her chin to meet my gaze. "Tell me anyway."

The brush of a smile lifted her lips and she began. "My father left the Brackish Wood a week before my sixteenth birthday, promising to return soon after with a gift. He said he'd bring something we didn't have. Something that grew in the human kingdoms."

I did know this story. I'd read her written rendition twenty times—a hundred times—but hearing it from her lips was a gift in itself.

"My mother stayed behind with me, overseeing the construction of the Brackish Castle. Even now I remember how silent she'd been. Cold and distant. I figured it was my father's leaving that had her snapping at anything I did or said right up to the day I turned sixteen, for she loved him more than anything in all of Revelry.

"The night of the next Cursed Moon was two days away when we received word of his death. He'd been traveling back to us with a single red rose as a gift to me. A storm had caught him, blowing him off course. He slammed into a tree and broke his neck. He should have known better than to shift in such weather, but he was trying to make it back to us on the night of my birthday. He was found a few days later with a single crumpled rose in his hand."

I stroked her hair as she retold the story of her beginning. Our childhoods had been so similar, so bereft of the love we needed. I'd been drawn to her from the first words on the page, just as I was drawn to her now, feeling her there on my chest, but also heavily in my heart.

"My mother withered away within days. The Cursed Moon came and went. She did not deliver any of the curses that had come from the Veil. I remember how they came to her. It was different for each Cursebringer over the centuries and hers came from a broken tree in the Brackish Wood. The Veil was thin there and she'd collect them between the pages of books. Each curse would settle into the words, waiting to be delivered." She paused, rubbing her temple. "It never made sense to me why she'd chosen such a vessel. Curses fit nicely into vials and jars, so why she'd chosen books of all things—and they were less common back then—I don't know."

"Someone's story within a story perhaps?"

She lifted her head with a grin. "You know, you might be right. That's very...whimsical. My mother used to think like that."

I pulled her up, nestling her head between my shoulder and jaw. "But your mother had hidden a curse. It remained undelivered on purpose."

"Yes," she breathed into my neck, tracing over the bare skin of my chest with one finger. "She met my father on the way to deliver his curse. Back then, it was a simple thing. He'd be cursed to meet a beautiful woman who would fall in love with him and he'd never know. He'd never be able to give her love."

"She knew it was her."

Reshina nodded. "She did. As soon as she saw him, she understood she was the beautiful woman. She was the one who would love him. And he would never give her love in return."

"So she hid the curse and fell in love with him anyway."

"Yes," Reshina sighed. "By the time I was born, she'd forgotten it. The curse grew and grew over a century. By the time they'd made me, it might as well have been a dream. All in her head.

"But after my father's death, she was a broken woman with no path to recovery. She blamed me for my father's death. Blamed me enough to go mad. One night, I slept in her room to watch over her. By then, the title of Cursebringer was dangerously close to becoming mine, and my mother was not done in her raging grief. She snuck away in the night while I slept and dug up the book where she had kept my father's curse.

"I still remember her face as she brought it to me. So pale and sallow as if my beautiful mother, who laughed in the rain, had shriveled into the corpse of someone I did not recognize. Her black eyes were furious, her voice low and full of pain. She asked me what I wanted most in the world right then.

"I could have said my father back. I could have said to be a family again. But all I could think of was the rose my father had traveled all through the night to deliver. I wanted it, not because it was beautiful, but because it was from him.

"When I told her a rose, it was already too late for me. She opened the book and the curse poured from its pages."

Reshina stilled, silent after recounting the tale. I kissed the top of her head. "The curse had grown."

"The curse had grown," she repeated in a heavy sigh. "Instead of being unable to love one person, I was cursed to never be able to love at all."

"And you cannot tell me how to break it."

Her hand wrapped around my chest. "And I cannot tell you how to break it. The curse will not allow it. My mother died three days later. I was the Goddess of the Ravenfae when she left this world. Cursebringer, too."

"And you were Goddessdamned good at it."

She laughed. "I was. Far more efficient than my mother. I collected the curses from the Veil through a ring I'd had made. That way, I needn't return to the Brackish Wood to collect them. I placed them into their vials and delivered them on time. Well," she chuckled, "most of them."

I threaded my fingers through her bare hand. "But you gave this ring to the next Cursebringer."

"I did. Korven wears it now. He uses it in the same way I did. He's very good at his title."

"He had a good teacher."

She nodded.

"He had a good mother."

She froze at my words. "He did not know a mother's love, Arthur. I could not give it to him."

"You looked out for him all the same." I stretched my body, turning to press it against hers. "Korven has many qualities. For one, he is...protective in nature. He must have learned that from you."

She grinned beautifully, her eyes lighting up in humor. "I see you truly have met him. Yes, Korven is protective of those he loves."

"I must admit if we ever meet again, I doubt it would be a warm welcome from him."

"You left on bad terms?"

I gazed off into the distance. "Let's just say, he didn't particularly enjoy my company and is in no hurry to see me again."

She grunted an agreement. "My children will be just fine without me. Where I could not love them, they found a special bond between themselves. They are very close and I don't doubt they will continue on to make their own families beautifully."

"For now, you have this family." I kissed her softly, squeezing her hand.

"You?"

"Me."

"And?"

"Master?" came a harsh whisper at the door.

"I think the other has just arrived."

She laughed into my neck as I answered Piffle. "She is awake!" I called. "You may come in!"

Piffle came around the corner of the archway, a hand over his eyes. "Will I be seeing all your bits and baubles out if I look?"

I pulled the sheets higher over our bodies. "We haven't gotten around to that part yet."

Reshina slapped my arm playfully and rolled out of my grasp, wrapping one of the sheets around her body.

"It is good to see you up again, Mistress," Piffle said with undying love for her in his voice. "Here, I've brought you some soup."

"She doesn't want soup, Piff!" I called, rising from the bed and slipping into my clothes. "The Mistress wants chocolate!"

"Ignore him," she said, taking the bowl of soup to the chair by the fire. "Thank you, Piffle. This smells divine."

"It's been simmering since dawn! I couldn't sleep, you see, with all the worries about you right here." He pointed to his chest, the little rake, and Reshina smiled so warmly, I wondered what I could say to get her to look at me like that.

"You are such a good friend. I'm sure I'll recover quickly with this meal."

Piff went about with a grin on his face, picking up things here and there, mumbling about all he'd seen and heard at the market. "They've decorated the town for the Sprouting Festival. The color this year is a beautiful lilac hue which wouldn't look very good on the Mistress, I'm afraid, so I didn't take the liberty of purchasing the annual fabric, though I did find a lovely shade of midnight blue. I was thinking it would make a daring two piece if I just add a few layers of that shimmery black fabric, you know the one I used for the bodice the Master ripped last week, and—"

"The festival is soon?" I paused washing my face, water dripping down my chin.

Piffle stilled, realization blooming in his eyes. He cleared his throat, pouring tea for Reshina. "It is, Master. I will acquire the necessary flowers at the next market visit. NOTEBOOK!" He shifted into his golden notebook where he kept all his lists, committing them to memory before he left for market. There he scratched his notes before popping back into a fae.

"What is the Sprouting Festival?" Reshina asked.

Piff glanced at me in the mirror before answering. "It is a celebration of spring in Heartstone, Mistress. The kingdom gathers in one color to celebrate the renewal of life. Gardeners sell their flowers at the market and people dance in the streets."

"It's also the anniversary of my mother's death," I added, wiping my face. "And of the curse coming upon me."

"I see."

"Well then,"—Piff cleared his throat—"I'll just be off to put out those chairs you asked for in the corridors, Mistress. I found that chocolate you liked, too. Shall I bring you some?"

She shook her head, watching me carefully. "No, Piffle, thank you. I'd love some later."

The little man bowed at the waist with another sharp glance in my direction before he left.

"Are you alright?" she asked softly.

"Fine."

She tried another approach. "Let me rephrase. This anniversary means something to you. Will you tell me about it?"

"It's nothing," I said, dismissing the conversation, placing a kiss on her forehead.

"It is quite obviously something. Please tell me."

I sank into the chair opposite of her. She had tucked the corner of the silky red sheet just beneath her underarm and it was in danger of slipping. I rubbed my mouth and looked away. "Every year, I bring flowers to my mother's grave on the anniversary of her death. I stand at her headstone for one hour, just as I stood at her bedside for that time watching her life leave her, waiting for the curse to take me as soon as it did. It is the one time of the year the Beast allows me the most control, though I am Beast all the same." I chuckled lightly, setting my elbows on my knees and leaning towards her for the spoonful of soup she offered. "The Beast agrees not to tear Piffle's head off when he joins me." I swallowed the soup, impressed at its flavors. "I'll have him look at the exact dates, but my guess is it will be in two weeks."

"I'm coming, too, this year."

My gaze shot to hers. "You certainly are not."

She sipped another spoonful, twisting the spoon in her mouth and pulling it across her lips. "I am."

"Reshina," I sighed. "I cannot guarantee the Beast wouldn't harm you. Again. It's too dangerous."

"You said we are family. Family supports each other through grief. I am coming."

She took another spoonful. Then another. Her dining habits

were so careful. Poised in a crimson bedsheet, the exhaustion of fever and sweat pressing wisps of her hair to her forehead, she still ate with a graceful touch. With each dip into the broth, she lightly pulled the spoon across the bowl so it couldn't drip on her lap. She brought it to her mouth where she savored it—truly enjoyed each mouthful.

"I love watching you eat," I admitted.

"Oh? And why is that?"

I slid off the chair, on my hands and knees, crawling to her. "You're the most graceful woman I've ever known. I've never had the pleasure of watching a Goddess sip soup draped in a sheet from my bed." I trailed a hand under the silk and up her leg, revealing her skin and kissing the top of her knee. "You know," I said, lifting her leg by the ankle and laying it across my back, "I don't think I've had the pleasure of watching a Goddess eat while she herself is..." I kissed the bite mark on her thigh, pulling a sigh from her lips. "Consumed."

I found her center with my tongue and the spoon dropped with a clatter into the bowl before her hands dragged through my hair. She gasped and I lifted her other leg across my back, pulling her to the edge of the seat.

Between the kisses, the sucking on her clit, and my fingers pulsing inside her, she still managed to speak. "I'm going to be there, you know," she panted between sharp inhales of breath. "I'll not be parted from you for it."

I growled against her inner thigh, nipping at her wound. She squeaked, laughing as I kissed over her belly, pulling away the rest of the sheet to reveal the body I'd been busy worshiping for months. "You're not going."

She grabbed my face, kissing me hard, all that desire from the bite, her fever, and my mouth, wild between us. She had my cock firmly in her grasp, lining herself up on the edge of the seat, guiding me inside. Her teeth pulled at my bottom lip with my first thrust deep within her. I moaned in relief, knowing I wouldn't last long this round. She pulled at my shoulders and I picked her up, pressing her body against the stone wall as I moved inside her.

"Yes, I am," she panted, her nails digging into the back of my neck as she pulled on my ear with her lips. "Yes. I. Am."

CHAPTER 41

Reshina

ALL THREE OF US STOOD IN THE SILENT SNOWFALL AT THE foot of Marianna's grave. Fourteen red roses laid in the snow, marking the years since her death and the beginning of Arthur's curse as the Beast.

Piffle sniffled into a handkerchief, and I wondered if it was for Marianna or Arthur that he mourned. It was the Beast there beside me, not the man I knew, but the monster brought from the Veil. I slid my hand across the Beast's claws at his side, holding them there, giving my presence, and giving what I could.

We didn't say a thing. By then, there was no need to. No words of mourning. No hopeful comfort in the passing of the woman Arthur had respected as his mother, but never truly loved. The Beast took a deep breath, releasing it into the frozen air, leaving a cloud in its wake.

Arthur and I had continued to argue about my presence at his mother's memorial, but a Goddess was a Goddess and when we wanted something, we were sure to have it.

The three of us stayed for an hour. My thoughts drifted to what it must have been like for Arthur, watching the rasping sickness take his mother and inevitably take his life away from him.

It wasn't any wonder he had begged me to stab a knife through his chest all those weeks—he'd had nothing to hope for. But he hadn't mentioned it in months, and I hadn't even begun to look for another way to leave. I leaned my head against the Beast's arm and he shifted slightly. He wouldn't hurt me. He wouldn't bite me—not now, not at the moment that mattered so dearly to Arthur.

When the hour was up and Piffle and I walked silently back inside, Arthur joined us a few minutes later, shifting from Beast to man as he came down the stairwell. I took him into my arms where we sank to the steps, and I held his head at my chest as he silently wept.

THE SOFT SCRATCH OF THE PEN WAS WHAT WOKE HIM. I was busy writing notes in the margins of what looked like his most prized possession by the condition of it. *Cursed Goddess of the Veil* lay flat before me, the spine cracked, the pages thumbed through so many times, they stood on end of their own accord, stiff with a few small tears.

This edition had a pale blue cloth cover, frayed at the edges and corners. It was small, something that could easily fit inside a pocket, and when I'd discovered it in his bedside drawer, I'd almost laughed aloud to see myself there.

Here was the part of me Arthur had known for years. It was the book that led us to this point where I was naked in his bed with three leftover bite marks from the Beast within him.

The moment I discovered his treasure, I'd begun reading the book, fascinated by his notes in the spaces between the pages and along the margins. He'd annotated many—the most I'd seen in any of his books. By the time I got to the heart of the story, I'd grabbed his fancy pen that held ink inside the barrel and had begun to add my own notes.

I knew he wouldn't be angry about it. He consistently left me his favorite books after seven months of being his captive—asking me to add to his annotations and then return them to him.

I finished my last note, eyeing him as he stirred, his beautiful hands searching across the bed beside him. I scooted closer, cleared my throat, and began to read. "It was on that morning that I had come to understand change. She is a vile thing, yet you cannot stop her. Not a root from digging through the soil, not a flower from budding before it blooms. So I did nothing the day he left me but recognize the change. I accepted it and kept on living. My life was not his to break, nor was his mine. Once two lovers, we were then nothing but the past tense of the word. And though we shared a child, we did not share what was important at that time to him. An undying, everlasting love for each other."

I lowered the book, crawling to him and sliding my legs around his torso. "You've written something here in the margins. Do you remember what you said?"

Arthur nodded, sliding his hands along my bare thighs and speaking low. "I would not have left her."

I mirrored his nod. "I would not have left her." I snapped the book shut, tossing it to the side, boxing him in beneath me with my arms. "Have you always loved me?"

"Yes," he breathed. "And no."

I raised a brow.

"Yes, I've always loved you. Your story. How you've woven your words in here." He tapped his chest. "But I did not love you then as I love you now."

"Arthur." My voice cracked and I froze, unable to do anything but listen.

"I loved you then, but I did not know the look of you. The way you hold yourself." His eyes narrowed and he shook his head. "The steps you take in this realm and the one above as if you've lived it all. As if this world belongs to you, not you to it, and your poise, Reshina. I am transfixed by the mere sight of you walking towards me."

I opened my mouth to speak, but his hand was there, covering my words. "The way you taste. I loved you then, but I did not know the sweetness on your skin or the luscious warmth of your blood. And the way you feel beneath my hands, so supple. So soft."

Those exact hands shifted across my skin, tracing the line of my jaw where he held my face in his palms. "Yes, I have loved you for years. And for months, I have understood what I felt then was a fraction of what I feel now. I am immortalized by you. One day, when our time is done, you will continue on in this life, and I will not."

I jerked away in a desperate vehemence, but he followed, rising and holding me still. "As you said, change is a vile thing, but there is good in change, too. Change brought back the meaning in my life. Change gave me someone to love—the same one I'd been writing to in the margins of my books all those years, so she could read them in my bed in the early morning hours."

"Don't do this," I begged, the first spill of a tear sliding down my cheek.

"I love you now and I loved you then. I will love you tomorrow and the next day and the next. Until I am dead, cold in my grave, and the stars cease to shine, I will love you. There will be no leaving, Reshina. I am by your side until the day my heart fails and it cannot beat in your name."

"I cannot—"

"I know." He pressed his forehead to mine. "I know, I know. I know you cannot love me." He lifted his head in a smile that could light the world had he not been trapped beneath it. "I love you regardless. I know that if you could love me, you would."

I froze.

I could not move.

I could not indicate a single release of breath or shift of my hands on his chest.

The curse had more power over me than just stealing the words from my lips. Not only was I unable to confess love, I could not show it. I could not reveal even the slightest hint of the truth in my heart.

I loved.

Of course, I loved.

The curse, meant for my father but bestowed upon me, was a diabolical thing. One of the worst I'd ever encountered in all my time as Cursebringer.

The *ability* to love had never left me.

The *words* did.

I could never say them.

Never write them.

Never show the truth of them to anyone, even my own children, just babes in my arms, looking up into my eyes as if I was all that mattered in the entire world.

Not even then.

Not now as I had come to love this man with my entirety.

Until he moved or spoke again, I was trapped within my own curse.

He searched my eyes for something. Anything. Any sign or hint of what I could have felt in another time when I was not cursed and neither was he. I stared blankly at him, screaming, rattling in my cage, begging for him to somehow see that I loved him back.

He smiled sadly. "You cannot love me. I know. And you cannot tell me how your curse is broken. I know that, too." He laughed without humor. "Perhaps one day, I'll break it without meaning to. I'll kiss your elbow at just the right spot and poof! You'll tell me how much you love me then."

I lifted my arm, pointing my elbow towards him. "Might as well try," I rasped.

He did laugh then, kissing it swiftly, leaving little trails of his lips. He took the other, doing the same, pressing me down into the bed, laughing with me. The curse had released me, sure that the moment of confession had passed.

He swept the hair back from my face. "I have enough love for the both of us, Reshina. I am yours for however long you'd like me to be."

Forever, I whispered in the reaches of my mind, taking his face in my hands and pouring whatever love I could into my kiss.

I CAUGHT HER ONE DAY AS I ALWAYS DID, FALLING through the land we now both called home and into the Underrealm. This landing took its toll—sending me right through a tall mirror which had been propped up in Reshina's rooms for the times when Piffle draped her in luxurious gowns.

The glass shattered beneath me, and I lifted Reshina, preventing her from kneeling on the shards. She pulled me over to find my shirt torn and the skin of my back flayed in glass.

"What an entrance, Arthur," she laughed, pulling out a rather large piece with gusto. I winced as she kissed my lips, tearing out another.

"This fall might be the death of me," I grunted.

"Nonsense. You're already healing. Just a few more and—"

"*Fuck.*" I grimaced as another shard left my skin. "Kill me now and take me out of my misery."

She snorted into my neck just the way I loved and kissed my shoulder. "There. Already healing over. No worse for wear."

I flipped her on her back, exploring her mouth, nipping at her lip. "If you'll not kill me, Goddess, then marry me."

Her mouth opened and shut half a dozen times before I went on. "Marry me. Make me your husband. Give me your hand and give me your mornings, your nights. Give me all the time between to call you my wife."

"You cannot possibly want—"

"Oh, but I do." I threaded my hands behind her head. "You need not say you love me. I do not ask for the impossible. I ask you to accept me as yours."

As if she was frozen, she stared, her eyes wide.

"Marry me," I whispered again. "Say yes."

"Yes."

I closed my eyes, pressing my forehead to hers. "The most beautiful sound I've ever heard."

WE WERE MARRIED ON A GRAY WINTER DAY OVER A YEAR after she came to me. Piffle ordained the ceremony. We held it in the library. Reshina dressed in a layered gown of black, sparkling in the low candlelight.

I do not know what I wore.

I do not know what I said or if I even combed my hair that morning—the only thing I was sure I'd done was tell her I would be her husband and love her for all the time I had left in this world.

I presented her with a ring I'd crafted myself—something I'd never done before, but needed to get right the first time. I'd spent months hiding the metalworking books I was reading from her —taking quick peeks at them when she was helping Piffle in the kitchen. Reading chapters in the dead of night while she slept soundly in our bed, her wings taking up so much of the space, I had little but a thin edge.

Crafting the actual ring was even more difficult. There were times she believed me to be on the surface as the Beast when in reality, I was in the pantry, carving away at the band. I worked to create the illusion of feathers into the gold, setting small diamonds into them to represent the silver tips of her wings—placing the perfect precious stone of black onyx at the center. Piffle brought it by my request from Riche in a cut called *marquise*. It was regal. It was bold. It was her.

As I'd placed it on her finger, Reshina had struggled through the wording of the ceremony, adjusting what she was supposed to say. I didn't even think twice about it, just steadied myself not to upheave the contents of my stomach on her perfectly polished pointed heeled shoes.

I made love to her so softly that night, she cried. And no matter my consoling, she would not stop, pouring all of her tears into wails of anguish. Of all the men who'd loved her over the centuries, I was the only one who'd promised not to leave her. And I meant it. She couldn't love me, but she could be with me and that was all I had to hope for in the world.

We spent months redecorating the corridors, cooking together, reading, dancing, writing our story in a draft I couldn't even look over without tears brimming in my eyes. Becoming her husband had softened my edges, redirected my purpose, and given me the simplest and honest truth—everything had been worth it to wake up each morning next to her.

Over a year after the curse had dragged her into the Under-realm, Reshina was mine. The Beast settled so calmly, so quietly, rarely roaming the surface, rarely speaking up as long as she was near, as if her presence was a comfort to us both.

She wrote dozens of letters to her children, tossing them into the fire, crumpling them, tearing them to pieces. She said she couldn't find a way to come back into their lives that would benefit them.

I held her when she cried then, too.

I lived each day loving her with the intrinsic fear that one day, our world would shatter. We did not have all the time we wanted. It was a finite thing to love a Goddess trapped in the Underrealm. Loved and happy, but trapped all the same.

When the shattering did come, it came through a mouse.

With golden fur and a long golden tail, Piffle climbed up my chair next to the fire in the library, so small, I didn't see him until he whispered in my ear.

"Master!" he squeaked, and I startled, snapping my book shut. "Do not alert the Mistress!"

My gaze darted to Reshina. She was bent over the latest book we'd been passing back and forth, writing notes and ideas about the story as we read the chapters together.

"Follow me!" Piffle-Mouse said, scurrying back down the side of the chair.

I rose and stretched, walking casually to her, placing a kiss on her head and murmuring something about tea and chocolate. She gave me a quick smile and nodded, returning to the book immediately.

My heart thundered in my chest. It wasn't like Piffle to shy away from announcing himself to her. He loved her too in his way, their friendship one I admired.

I closed the library doors behind me to find the little Changlingfae ready to burst into tears. "It's all my fault!" he cried. "I should never have sent the letter! I should not have done it!"

I sat on the bench along the wall, careful in my next words. "What letter did you send?"

He began to pace back and forth across our new red carpeting. "One the Mistress meant for the fire. She'd been so wrought with it, you see, and tossed it carelessly. But it missed the flames and I couldn't help but pick it up and by then I was reading her words and, OH!" He buried his face in his hands, sobbing uncontrollably.

"Piff," I soothed, "if you sent one of Reshina's letters to whom I think you did, why are you telling me now?"

"Because she's here!" he squealed, eyeing the library doors when he realized how loud he'd been. "She's right outside the gates to Heartstone! She's begging to see the Mistress! It's all wrong! All gone wrong!"

I stood on solid feet, taking his shoulders into my hands. "Listen to me. *Who* is at the gates, Piff?"

He stuttered on his next breath with guilt across his brows. "It is Seraphine DuPont, sire. The mistress's daughter-in-law and Prince Korven's wife!"

HUNT. KILL.

"No. None of that."

BLOOD. HUNGER.

"You don't need those things anymore."

ALWAYS NEED. BRINGER?

"She is below. Safe. But this is important, Beast. You must try to let me speak through you again."

I peered through the eyes of the Beast, finding the spot of red at the black gates. Seraphine's blood raced through her veins despite the bitter cold.

"Where is she!" her voice called, echoing across our lands as the Beast approached. The unfamiliarity struck somewhere deep inside. I'd hardly heard her voice when we'd met over a decade before. "I need to speak with the Ravenfae Goddess Reshina! Or Arthur! Get Arthur! Please! He'll know who I am, *please*, if you have any sense of what I'm saying...to...you..."

Her words trailed as the Beast stood fully before her. She took a step back, far enough from the fence that he wouldn't be able to reach her through the bars. Even through the Beast's muted color in his vision, I could see that she was just as beautiful as the day I'd intended to save her all those years ago. Her now pointed ears told me she'd somehow become fae. Another story for another time, perhaps.

I urged my voice through the Beast. "SPEAK."

Her chest rose and fell rapidly in her cloak, the hem soiled in inches of mud. "I must speak with Reshina. It is imperative that I do so. Now."

"WHY." I'd meant it as a question, but the tone did not deliver.

Seraphine wrapped her arms around her chest, her face crest-fallen. "She must know the condition of her daughter, Morella. We,"—her eyes darted across the snow behind me, flickering over the walls of the gray stone castle—"need her help."

She bolted to the gate, wrapping her fingers around the frozen posts. "Please! Her life is in danger! We've tried every-thing! We've been searching for Reshina for *weeks*. Her daughter needs her, please, please let her go!"

"CANNOT."

Seraphine's face flared in rage as she rattled the bars. "Then bring her to me! Or allow me passage to that castle and I will speak to her!" In an uncharacteristic fit, she banged on the bars of the gate, kicking at the metal until it clanged. "If you do not allow me through, I will find a way through myself!"

In a flash of skirts, she turned, running along the edge of the fence. "Reshina!" she screamed. "Reshina!"

"Let her through," I urged.

BLOOD. SWEET. NEW.

"If you let her through, I will speak to Reshina about letting you bite her again."

BITE BRINGER.

"Yes, now open the gate!"

I knew he warred with the idea, thinking correctly that it was a lie. But he did as I asked, allowing me to call out to Seraphine. "ENTER."

She skidded to a stop, splattering more mud along her skirts and cloak. The Beast reached the gate and lifted it off its hinges, swinging it open with ease. With admirable caution, she stepped through, keeping her distance.

"BELOW," I explained.

"Can you show me the way?"

"YES."

The Beast trudged forward, the snow hitting his knees where it came up to Seraphine's hips. She followed behind his wake, her teeth chattering loudly.

When we reached the entrance to the Underrealm, I made the Beast speak once more. "STAY."

The Beast descended the stairs and in the transformation, she gasped. When I turned, her hands were over her mouth, realization, panic, and tears in her eyes. "Arthur?"

I held my hand out to her at the last step. "Come, Seraphine. I will take you to my wife."

CHAPTER 43

Reshina

THE AIR CHANGED THE MOMENT ARTHUR WALKED INTO the library because he didn't walk. He eased. I looked up at the sound of the door opening as I finished my latest annotation. We'd been sharing a mystery book, told from the point of view of the feline that had witnessed a murder. Most of our annotations had been plays on words of the feline nature and I was just finishing up my note about how at six-hundred pages, I thought this could be a shorter tail, when I looked up to see the tight lines of his face.

I rose from my chair immediately. "What is it?"

His lips parted to speak, yet nothing came.

I rushed to him, my skirts of a dark emerald trailing behind me. I touched his cheek, brushing my thumb across the fine growth of hairs he hadn't bothered to shave this morning due to keeping him between my legs. "You're frightening me," I rasped in a half laugh. "Tell me what is wrong."

Taking my hands into his, he closed his eyes, squeezing them shut as he kissed over my knuckles and my ring. "Someone is here."

"What do you mean *here*?"

"I mean just outside this door. She has come a long way to find you."

Morella, I thought, my heart jumping through my chest. *My daughter has come to find me.*

I didn't understand his hesitancy and tenderness in that moment, but I didn't take the time to try either. I left his side, rushing to the doors and opening them wide. There, in the long corridor we'd recently redecorated in shades of dark crimson, was Seraphine DuPont.

She was pacing outside of the door, half drenched in mud, her long golden hair braided down her back, falling out in pieces that draped around her face. Those bright violet eyes darted to me, and she stilled as if stunned.

My pulse raced as I swallowed my biggest fears. "Korven?" I whispered, thinking she'd come to tell me some horrible truth about my son.

She stood straight before me, lifting her trembling chin and giving me a short shake of her head. "It's Morella," she trembled. "Your daughter's life is in danger. You *must* come and save her."

MY WIFE LISTENED IN SILENCE. ANY OTHER WOULD HAVE thought she was taking the news well as Seraphine related what she'd told me on the way to the library. But I knew her. The slump in her wings. The stiffness in her neck. When Reshina refused to abide by the rules set in place before her, that was when she was most fragile. Not fragile like a rose, but fragile like the lighted fuse of an explosion.

When Seraphine explained the sickness, I knew right away what it was. It was not just the role of a Goddess of the Veil to look after her people, but also to heal them and give her essence from the Veil for them to thrive.

Morella was with child, we'd learned, and appeared to fare with the same sickness Reshina had suffered when she was pregnant with her. They'd been searching for Reshina for weeks without end, getting word out, desperate to uncover what had happened to the Goddess of the Ravenfae. And it wasn't until Piff had overheard something about it in the marketplace that he'd sent that letter to Korven—the one Reshina had never meant to send telling where she'd been.

"The sooner we leave, the better chance Morella has," Seraphine explained. "Korven and Killian are already there, doing everything they can. They've called in the best healers of Revelry." Seraphine stepped forward, taking one of Reshina's hands into hers. "She needs you. We all need you. When your letter came, I opened it secretly. I couldn't give hope to Korven or Killian until I knew what it contained. I recognized your handwriting and you can imagine my surprise to find you'd ended up here. With Arthur." She nodded towards me. "Please come. I shifted through the trees to find this place. They think I've gone to another healer in the Citrine Cliffs." She took Reshina's other hand. "I will bring you back, I promise. Korven will understand...with time...why you've chosen to stay."

"You think I chose to stay here for over a year?"

The cut of her words hit me solidly, like a heated knife across my skin. I knew what she meant, but the way we'd been living as if we were free from the outside world was suddenly a burn on my heart—a lie we'd fashioned together.

"You disappeared!" Seraphine cried. "We thought you'd chosen another life!"

"I have been trapped inside a curse I delivered here decades ago. I cannot leave. The curse does not allow it."

Seraphine's lip trembled again. "Give me your hand. I'll shift us away from here right now." She pulled Reshina to the wooden bench along the wall. So Seraphine was a Forestfae then, able to move herself and others across the land through the wood of the trees of Revelry.

Seraphine gripped the armrest, squeezing her eyes shut. When nothing happened, she groaned in exasperation, pacing again. "I know all curses can be broken. What must be done to break this one?"

I stepped forward. "There is a way."

"No." The snap of Reshina's word resounded through the corridor.

I reached for her, pulling her to me. "I told you it would come to this."

"NO!" She yanked her hand from mine, backing away. "The curse cannot be broken," she muttered, her eyes frantic.

I followed her, softly pinning her against the tapestry along the stone wall. "You can do this," I breathed. "You must go. You'll never forgive yourself if you don't."

"You are wrong, Arthur," she said with ire. "I. Cannot. Do. This."

"Look at me." She turned her head, squeezing her eyes shut in refusal. "This is not the end. Do you remember what I said?" She shook her head, tears streaming freely down her face. "I said I have been immortalized by you. All of this,"—I stroked her cheek, gently turning her back to me—"all of it was real. And I have loved you—" My voice broke. But I'd not been through years of torment and months of bliss just to fall apart when the time came to be strong for her. I swallowed all of it down. "So much. It's time for you to go. Save your daughter. Enjoy your grandchildren and children and don't forget to take care of Piffle along the way."

"Fuck you," she seethed, grabbing my face. "I said *no*."

She shifted between my arms, soaring down the corridor without another word.

"Fuck," I heaved, already feeling the heat of the Beast's blood pulsing through my veins in the shift.

Seraphine twirled around. "Is she going to try to leave?"

"No," I called, racing down the corridor after her. "She's going to try for the western corridor!"

CHAPTER 45

Reshina

I SOARED THROUGH THE GREAT HALL ON BORROWED time. I would not allow my daughter to die. I would not kill my husband. When all the paths were laid bare, and I was stripped of any sense of normalcy, of safety, I chose proactivity. It had been that way all my centuries. I'd always fought back to it. And I'd always won.

But this...this I did not know how to manage. There was no choice I could make except to find the one Goddess in the Underrealm who could help me in a way I could not forsee.

I slowed my wings, flapping into the dark of the western corridor, shifting back to Ravenfae when my feathers brushed along the narrow walls. The Beast followed me, but I didn't care. I'd get through these tunnels with bite marks, drained of blood—whatever it took to reach Ishtak.

I misjudged the Beast. It had been so long since I'd truly run from him that I had forgotten how swiftly he could close the distance between us. The clicking began, alerting me that the Underfae dwelled near. I'd stun as many creatures as I could and rely on unrelenting rage for the rest.

The sharp claws of the Beast grabbed hold of my wings, yanking me back just as an Underfae brushed across my leg. I screamed in rage and fear, desperate to get to the end of that tunnel, desperate for someone to save me from what would come at too great a cost.

Arthur pinned me to the cavern wall, his shift from the Beast slowly forming over his body. "I won't let you," he heaved. "They will kill you."

"What if we go together?" I pleaded in the dark, touching his arms, his neck, his face, desperate for more of him, needing so much more.

He shook his head. "It won't work. I cannot tell you why."

Ishtak had his explanation sealed, just as she'd hidden the truth of the Underfae from the world above.

To my horror, he slipped a long dagger into my palm, kissing my knuckles and squeezing my fingers around the hilt. My hand shook as he lined it up at his chest. "Do it and know that I love you."

"I *hate* you," I cried, preparing to shift beneath him. "You are my husband, and you will stay my husband, and I will save my daughter, and Ishtak can—"

"You've never asked me about my scar."

My breath shuddered on the inhale, and I swallowed hard. "Do not do this."

"I was ten."

I shook my head angrily. "I do not wish to hear!"

"My father took a good look at me one day in passing, seeing my mother's face, knowing she loved her son, but not his father."

"Arthur please, I'm begging you—"

"The Beast struck in a bloody rage before I had a chance to run. And though my face was forever marred that day, my mother's became unrecognizable. Shredded to the point where our only resemblance was in the brutality of him."

My lips trembled and tears streamed down my cheeks. I felt for the line of tight skin that ran from his temple to the base of his jaw. "Why are you telling me this?"

He pulled my palm to his lips. "Because I need you to know that I am accustomed to the pain. I have known loneliness. I have known sorrow, even in my youth. They've been the dread in my thoughts and the shadows in the corners of my rooms for years, biding their time to send me to madness—just like my father before me."

Wrapping a hand around the back of my neck, he pulled me closer, the tip of the knife barely piercing his skin. "But you, Goddess. You became my savior. First through the lines of a book. Then in the flesh and blood, spilling onto my lands to save me from a cruel and dire fate. I would take this dagger to my chest a hundredfold if it meant these last months were real. That you were real."

I wrapped my hand around his—desperately grabbing onto the comfort of his fingers through mine. "You cannot ask me to do this."

"You are the Goddess of the Ravenfae. Your daughter's life is hanging by a thread. You have no other choice. You will do what needs to be done. So do it."

"I. *Can't*," I seethed through my teeth, attempting to escape his grip on my hand holding the knife.

"Then I will do it for you."

I screamed in agony as he jolted forward, forcing his body upon the blade, his hand—his beautiful, strong hand—gripping mine so tightly, I'd find bruises left from his fingers.

"I've loved you for so long," he grunted, easing his body closer to me with more of the blade sliding into his chest. Before the steel was buried through his heart completely, he pressed a kiss to my lips, leaving a smear of blood and whispering, "And I will see you again beyond the Veil."

My hand warmed as his blood trickled down my knuckles. His lips were still held to mine as he began to fall, and the weight of the curse holding me to the Underrealm lifted in an audible sigh, breezing through the tunnel.

But it wasn't the only one.

The curse that had plagued me for over five hundred years broke from my soul. Like shattered glass, I bellowed a scream not of this realm. A flood of all I'd never been able to say poured from my mouth as if my body retched with words of the unyielding love I'd felt since I was a sixteen year old child.

"*I love you, I love you, I love you!*" I screamed into his chest, as he lay on the floor. I tore at his shirt pooling in crimson stains. "COME BACK TO ME! I LOVE YOU!"

He believed I didn't.

And he sacrificed his life for me anyway.

Self-sacrifice of one's life was a cruel and unusual way to break my curse, but the harshness of it mirrored the outlines of the curse, and when he'd held my hand steady and pinned himself upon the blade, he'd broken both of them. One from a blade through the heart, held by my hand. One through the sacrifice of love.

I cursed the realm, the Veil, the stars in the sky as I shoved my hands in my pockets, not stopping to swipe the tears streaming down my face. "*Where is it, where is it?*" I laid the vials of undelivered curses out on the rocky floor, my hands shaking, touching each one, searching for the exact bottle I needed. They glowed in colors of red and green and pink, illuminating the dark.

It could work, I told myself. *It had to.*

The glass vials clinked together until I touched the one I needed. I yanked the cork from the opening and tilted my head back, breathing in the crimson smoke as six seeds of pomegranate trickled onto my tongue. I crushed them in my teeth, barely registering the sharp tartness of the juice. I lined my fingers along the side of Arthur's throat, feeling for any sign of a pulse. It was so faint, I knew I had no time. I kissed his lips as soon as the seeds were down my throat, searching for his pulse again.

"Mistress!" Piffle howled down the dark tunnel, followed by the calls of Seraphine.

I ignored them, relying on Piffle to keep her from entering too far. "Please, Arthur, stay here with me."

I counted the timing of his heart. Twenty-two. Twenty-two beats in one minute. The King of Heartstone was on the brink of death, but as I continued to press my ear at his chest and press my fingers to his neck, his pulse kept its slow, steady rhythm. It wouldn't be enough to wake him, but enough to keep him from the Veil—especially now that he was bound to me.

Bright light from a candle lit the tunnel and Piffle treaded carefully towards us, Seraphine in tow.

"He's not dead. He will not wake, but I can leave him for now."

"But how have you—"

I cut Piffle off. "There's no time to explain it. Seraphine, can you sift us to Morella?"

"I can."

I reached for her hand. "Piffle, keep this candle alight and stay with him. Manage his blood as best you can. I will be back soon."

The Changlingfae screamed. "There's a knife in his chest!"

"And it must stay there for now. Keep the light on him and the Underfae will stay back. I will save him, Piff. I promise that to both of us."

He cried silently, sitting down next to his master. The wound at Arthur's chest had ceased its bleeding, leaving him in a state of dwindling time.

"I'm ready," I said, squeezing Seraphine's fingers. She nodded and raced with me back down the corridor.

I led her to the dining hall, where she placed her hand on Arthur's chair and for the first time in thirteen months, I left the confines of Heartstone Castle and the Underrealm below.

CHAPTER 46

The Beast

STAY.

...

STRONG.

STAY.

LIVE.

...is she...free...?

BRINGER. GONE.

Let...her...go.

CANNOT HUNT HER.

STAY.

Goodbye...old...friend.

SERAPHINE SIFTED US FROM THE CHAIR TO A TREE outside, then to the wheel of an old carriage. As a Forestfae, she would be the fastest mode of travel all the way across Revelry to the Citrine Cliffs.

I observed that she was tired or still new to her fae powers as with each sift the distance was shorter and her breathing labored. Thirty minutes later, the gold of the Citrine Cliffs shimmered before us.

I set aside the gnawing at my heart. Arthur was still alive. I'd know if he wasn't. With the rogue curse I'd taken, I'd be bound to the next person I kissed for six months of the year, forced to remain in their presence for at least half the hours of each day. Arthur was alive when I'd kissed him, and so, the curse was keeping his heart beating, but it would not wake him, and I feared the strength of the calling Veil over the power of the curse.

When at last Seraphine tumbled us through an old door carved in trees and mushrooms, she fell onto the floor in a loud thunk, sprawled out across a blue woven rug.

"Seraphine!" My son raced from the enormous bed in the room, diving to the floor, picking his wife up into his arms. She moaned, curling into his chest. He finally looked my way, disbelief crossing his face. "Mother?"

"Korven," I choked. "There isn't time to explain. Where's Morella?"

"She is here." An enormous man rose from the bedside with lightly freckled skin and wild blue eyes, rimmed red. His copper hair fell into his face where a scruffy beard covered his chin and cheeks. "Tell me you can save her," he pleaded.

"Killian?" I guessed.

He nodded, crossing the room in two strides and taking my arm, leading me to the bed. There my daughter lay over shimmering wings of gold. Her face had sunken, cheeks no longer round, lips no longer plump and red. I pressed a hand to her forehead, recognizing the high temperature.

"How long has she been like this?"

Killian answered me, resuming his bedside vigilance. "Forty-one days and five hours." He pulled back the blankets over her belly, revealing a budding round shape. "She's five months along with our child."

I placed my hand over her, closing my eyes and reaching for the babe. As the Ravenfae Goddess of the Realm, I could find every single one of them. If I concentrated hard enough, I'd feel every Ravenfae life source from the Veil. I breathed a sigh. "Your child is alive and well."

Killian tore his hands through his hair, rocking in his agitation. "And Morella? What can you do for her?"

"I need you to leave."

"No," he snapped.

"Korven," I called, "escort your wife and Morella's husband from this room."

Killian bolted out of his chair. "I will not leave her!"

"You will if you want her to live, now go. She has no time for this."

"Who do you—"

Korven turned him by the shoulders. "I know you don't understand, but you need to listen to her. Please. Help Seraphine. She shifted too hard and needs to rest. I promise I will not leave Morella."

Killian's eyes darted to me in a sharp glare. The man didn't trust his wife's mother, whom he'd never met. That alone told me he was a good husband.

"Alright," he conceded. "I will not leave this room for long." He leaned down, sweeping a hand over Morella's forehead. "Moh Geràdah, Moh Dóches," he whispered as he kissed her. Turning to Seraphine, he draped her arm over his shoulder and left the room.

"What can you do?" Korven asked quickly.

"Sit there," I ordered. His brow raised, but he did as I said, sitting on the opposite side of his sister.

"When I was carrying her, I got sick. It's part of why it took me so long to return to the Brackish Wood and get back to you that summer."

He nodded silently, pulling his sister's hand into his. "It is a sickness that I've only seen in Ravenfae mothers. Our people are the Cursebringers, the race of fae tied most closely to the Veil, and we hold within us memories of our time before we crossed over to this realm. With her child from the Veil growing inside her, the Veil is thin around Morella. She comes from a long line of Cursebringers and was originally born to become one."

He frowned, his dark eyes furrowed. "You're saying I've done this to her? By taking the role of Cursebringer?"

"No. I have by being away for so long." I swept my hand over her cheek. "Keep her hand in yours. Just as the Goddesses did for me when I had this illness, we will take her hands and pull her back from the edge of the Veil, and remind her she is needed here. We will pour everything into it. All our good memories. All our love for her."

"Your *love* for her?" He searched my face. "You love Morella?"

"Yes," I laughed. "And you."

"Your curse—"

"Has been broken."

His deep brown eyes limned with tears. "Right. You'll explain later. I just—are you sure it's broken?"

"I've always loved you and your sister. Only now I can say it. Now I can show it." I pulled him closer, wrapping my arms around him, telling him again, "I never meant to hurt you."

He sniffed, composing himself, weary of my confession. "I trust you, mother."

We took Morella's hands in ours, eyes closed, searching for her spirit.

I brought forth memories of holding her in my arms as a babe. Of watching her brother hold her hand as she learned to walk, knowing how dearly I loved them both. I brought my thoughts closer to the present, watching her sign the contract to be married when she was but fifteen years old, curious if she'd choose to work her way out of it by the time the marriage date neared.

The tug on her spirit was sharp. Korven was finding his sister there too, close to the shadow of the Veil. We pulled together, he and I, each of us taking a side. Her spirit was golden, a brilliant light against the dark and with one final memory, she tumbled back with us from the shadows of the Veil.

Through a gasp of air, her eyes flew open, wide and confused.

"Thank the fucking Goddessdamned stars, Morella," Korven breathed. "Are you alright?"

"What happened? Where am—" Her focus caught mine. "... Mother?"

Her eyes of honey gold widened. "Mother!" She sat upright, throwing her arms around my neck. I held her there, reaching out to pull Korven into the embrace, both of my children back in my arms again where I could love them fully.

KILLIAN SOON BURST THROUGH THE DOOR AND SHOVED everyone aside except the guard who had returned with him. The Changlingfae had rich brown skin and fingers tipped in gold, one baby cradled in the crook of his arm, and my granddaughter hanging off his back. After they spoke quickly, the man handed the children off to their parents, and I stepped aside to meet my newest granddaughter.

"Her name is Elryci. We call her El for short."

I took her into my arms, cradling her there and feeling the telltale warmth of love wash over me. "Hello, El." I kissed her forehead, taking a moment to glance around the room.

Killian and the man I assumed to be his closest advisor still hovered over Morella, who was clearly telling them to get a grip and let her breathe.

I handed El back to Seraphine. "I have to go."

"But you've just arrived." Korven set his firstborn down onto the ground where she quickly sprinted to the bed, climbing on top and diving into Morella's arms.

A smile tugged at his lips, but fell when he continued. "You've explained nothing. You've been gone for a year. A *year*, mother. An entire fucking year, and—"

I held a hand up between us. "I must get back to Arthur. I have to save him." I turned to Killian. "Can you take me to Heartstone Castle? Fast as you can?"

He glanced at Morella who nodded. "Yes."

"Who is Arthur?" Korven fumed.

"*Korven*." There was a warning in Seraphine's voice.

"Wait just a Goddessdamned minute," he continued, slipping a hand through his hair. "*Arthur*? *Duke-of-fucking-Riche, Arthur*?"

"Like I said, I will explain everything upon my return."

"In what, another year? Two?"

Korven!" Seraphine yanked his arm. "Arthur is her *husband*. She loves him."

His glare towards me could have killed a man, but not a Goddess, and before he could say another word, I held my hand out to Killian. With his touch on the headboard, we were gone.

KILLIAN PLACED ME OUTSIDE THE GATES OF HEARTSTONE Castle within five minutes, grunting a quick apology before sifting away again. I shifted and flew through the light snowfall, flying into the entrance of the Underrealm, finding the great hall, and sweeping down the western corridor. I soon reached Piffle who huddled over Arthur's body.

"Has anything changed?"

"No, Mistress. He is breathing, but this..." He gestured to the knife protruding from his chest. "Is there hope?"

I nodded, rising to my feet. I slipped off my shoes and pinned my hair back into place. "He is not leaving us. Now help me turn him."

"But that is the wrong way, Mistress!" he shouted as I grabbed the fabric of Arthur's shoulders, pointing him towards the deepening dark.

"It is the right way, Piffle. It's time we visit a Goddess."

The Beast

BRINGER.

...

SHE HAS COME.

...Re...

BRINGER HAS COME. DOWN TO DARKNESS.

the... Under... fae...

SHE PULLS US. THEY COME.

No... stop... her...

BRINGER STRONG. POWERFUL.

Reshina... wait...

ISHTAK NEAR.

Stop her.

MOTHER APPROACHES.

Reshina

PUSHING ASIDE HOW MUCH I HATED IT, I PULLED THE dagger from Arthur's chest, instructing Piffle to bandage over the wound. While the cut stopped bleeding, he could not close it, and after attempting three times, I instructed him to stop. He held the candlestick while I pulled under Arthur's arm, slowly dragging his body further through the tunnel. Piffle followed in quiet whimpers, cowering at the Underfae who came near, their clicks preceding them. But I was now a Goddess without limits.

The first came, springing from the dark and I stunned it. Piffle's light caused the others to hiss and sink back into the crevices of the tunnel.

I searched their faces and features for the one we had captured, finding her peering out at us curiously, *hungrily*, from a rocky crevice. I addressed her, stunning those around her, though more were coming. "I will give my blood freely, but you must tell the others to let us pass!" I spoke with clarity, our eyes meeting in the dim. She emitted a few clicks as if trying to communicate with me. I cut my arm with the dagger and she slid closer, eyeing me carefully. "I will leave a trail for you. For all of you, but you must allow us passage to Ishtak. If you cannot abide by this bargain, I will start removing your heads from your necks."

She clicked once, darting to the dripping of blood below my arm. Licking the rock furiously, she clicked again several times. I chose to trust her for that moment, releasing the spell over the others. She communicated to them again, and without wasting time, I continued dragging, slicing into my arm every few minutes as the wound closed. Soon, I knew my bargain had been accepted. Soon, a long trail of a Goddess's blood stained the tunnel behind us, dozens of Underfae in tow with their faces pressed to the rocky floor.

"Ishtak! I seek Ishtak, Goddess of the Underfae!" I yelled, grunting and pulling my husband's body in great heaves. I kneeled down to Arthur, checking his pulse again. "Please! Ishtak!" My voice echoed endlessly through the cavern, my arms bloody and the coppery scent permeating the increasingly putrid stench of the tunnel.

"Just a bit more, Mistress," Piffle whispered. "Just a bit more and we can reach her."

I nodded, swallowing my fears. After what felt like hours, the stone floor transitioned into smooth marble, crusted over with something black and flaking. My bare feet slapped against it as the tunnel opened into a low-lit cavern.

The clicking of the Underfae echoed on the rounded walls, shaded in shadows. I pulled Arthur further into the room, bending down beside him, cradling his head in my lap. "Ishtak?" I heaved, catching my breath.

A voice came from the dark. "Is that you, Reshina? Ravenfae Goddess of the Veil?"

I cried in a sigh of relief. "Yes, Ishtak, it's me."

She entered the light of Piffle's candle and I bolted upward. Where once I knew an old woman with silver hair, pale skin, and grey eyes now a corpse stood before me. Bite marks spread all over her body, mottling her once pale skin to purple and black stretched over sharp bones. She wore a simple dress of black, tattered and frayed with slashes throughout the material.

Furious, I cast my gaze to the Underfae crawling up the walls, their incessant clicking inciting my anger further. "What have they *done* to you?"

Ishtak hobbled forward. "No more than I've allowed them to do."

I swallowed my questions and my ferocity at seeing a Goddess of the Veil in such condition. "I need your help. My husband is dying and I do not know how to save him."

She shuffled forward, peering down at Arthur, his chest barely moving. "The King of Heartstone Castle has returned where he vowed never to return again."

"Great Goddess of the Underfae!" Piffle cried. "Oh, Dark Mistress of the Underrealm! He does not return of his own free will! We have dragged him here! He does not know!"

"Tell me," I demanded. "Tell me what has been done to your faekind."

Though her body stood crippled, her eyes darted to me in sharp anger. "You have no power here, Reshina, Goddess of the Ravenfae. No authority to ask such things."

I swept my hand in an arc, stunning the Underfae creeping closer along the walls. They stilled, frozen. "I have every authority. You've done something to them. I know it to be true."

Her beady black eyes narrowed.

"But I care not," I continued. "I am here, begging you to save *him*."

"I saved him once already."

"*How?*"

She bent on cracking knees and I followed, refusing to trust her so close to the man I loved. With bony fingers, she pulled back the tatters of his shirt. Her eyes squinted to slits as she looked over the wound, tracing the flayed skin. "Ah," she cackled, "There he is."

"Who?"

"The Beast."

In a split moment he shifted, transforming before us. With fur indistinguishable from black in the dim light, the Beast's chest heaved and he turned, a low growl rumbling from his throat.

"But the curse…" I trailed. "The curse was broken. I was able to leave. Why is the Beast still with him?"

Ishtak slowly rose, her eyes filled with greed. "You have returned to this place, Beast. Do you remember the cost?"

A dark voice I'd never heard rumbled from his chest. "YES, MOTHER."

"Mother?" I took a step back, pulling Piffle behind me. "Explain yourself."

A dark grin lifted her lips. "When the curse you delivered upon this land settled into its king, he fell into the Underrealm. My realm. I knew the father, but the son was…different."

She slid her hand over the Beast's arm and I darted forward, snatching it into mine. "You will refrain from touching my husband, Ishtak."

"This Beast is not your husband."

I dropped her hand. "*Every* part of him is my husband."

Her low cackle set my teeth on edge. "My children would have killed your Arthur had I not intervened after he fell. They'd almost drained him dry, hadn't they, Piffle?"

The Changeling fae nodded, clinging to my skirts.

"What did you do to him?" I whispered.

"I bound him to my realm by way of the Beast inside, forcing him to feed my children in exchange for saving his life."

"Feed your…" I searched the walls. Hundreds of Underfae crawled along them, leering over us as one hoard. "The biting. The hunting. The obsession with blood… the Beast was hunting to feed *them?*"

"The sustenance my children seek was delivered here

through the Beast. He drank the blood of animals and it nourished their bodies through a power given to me as Goddess of the Underfae. He was their brother." She lifted her arms, twisting them to show the bruised bite marks all through her skin. "I assume you are the reason he has not been hunting and I have become their primary source of food."

"Ishtak," I whispered. "How have the Underfae become... this?"

Her head lowered. "It is a long tale. For another time, perhaps."

I shoved my questions aside, coming to one conclusion. "Arthur didn't know the Beast hunted for the Underfae."

"He did not."

"And what is the cost of him returning here?"

Her eyes met mine. "Death of the man inside the Beast."

I moved swiftly, positioning myself between her and the Beast, the dagger drawn, pointed right between her ribs. "You will save his life, not take it."

Her laugh echoed around us, madness seeping from her acrid breath. "You cannot harm me, Ravenfae Goddess."

"No. But your children are not safe in my presence." Before she could stop me, I threw a vial from my pocket. It hit the cavern ceiling, shattering with silver smoke pouring over her children, the distant sound of music chiming through the cavern.

"NO!" she screamed, sprinting faster than I would have thought possible as they began to fall, one after the other after the other. Bones snapped and her screaming continued.

"Be ready to leave quickly," I said to Piffle, who nodded rapidly, sticking close to the Beast, still prone on the floor with labored breaths.

"Curses are never delivered to the Underfae, Ishtak, now why is that?" I picked up the hem of my skirts, taking slow, deliberate steps toward her and her children broken on the floor. "What questions the Goddesses of the Veil might ask... What interest they might have if I care to tell them the tale of my visit to you."

"What have you done to them!" she screamed.

The Underfae that had fallen lay before her, knocked unconscious but alive.

"Heal him. Allow us passage through this corridor, and I will leave a letter at the entrance detailing their curse."

"And how to break it?"

"Yes."

"The Beast must stay," she demanded. "He must continue to roam the land of Heartstone and drink the blood he craves to feed my children."

"For three months of the year."

"Six."

"Done."

She rose from the floor and I counted the Underfae the curse had captured. Twelve of her children lay sprawled across the flecks of black, which I'd come to realize was dried blood. The change over them had already begun and it became more imperative that we leave as quickly as possible.

Ishtak made quick work of the vein at her wrist, biting into her skin, ripping flesh and allowing a stream of her dark blood to pour into the Beast's maw.

She stepped back as he stirred. "Go. Do not repeat what you have seen." She flicked her hand toward Piffle. "He will not be able to speak about it and your husband will not remember it. Do not seek me out again, Reshina."

"No, Ishtak. When the time comes, it is you who will seek me."

With the last of my words, the Beast had released himself back to Arthur, his wound closed, his chest steadily breathing. I pulled him up to sit, taking one of his arms over my shoulder. His head leaned on mine, his eyes closed as if he was stumbling around in a dream.

With the guidance of Piffle's candlelight, we trekked down the corridor one last time. The Underfae gave us a wide birth, but watched carefully with their eyes of black, sharp fangs glinting in the light.

When we made it through the entrance and finally stepped back into the great hall, Arthur stumbled, falling onto the black marble floor. His eyes blinked open, focusing on my face. "Another dream?"

I laughed, allowing my tears to stream freely. With hands caked in blood, I brushed the golden hair from his forehead. "No. No, it is not, but I must tell you something."

He blinked again, tears pooling in his eyes.

I kissed his lips soft and slow. "I love you," I whispered there, drawing back to watch his face.

With shaking hands, he cupped my cheeks. "It is a dream, then."

I laughed in half a sob, taking one of his strong hands and biting down hard on his palm.

He hissed in pain and bolted upright with narrowed eyes, darting over my face, my body, meeting my eyes of dark brown to his steel blue. "You love me?"

I nodded repeatedly, working my way into his lap, pulling him to me—the truth of everything I wanted to say finally at the tip of my tongue, but I could not say it through the tremble of my chin. Instead, I chose to say the simplicity of it again. "I do, Arthur. I love you."

He pulled my mouth to his and our kiss was wild between us —the same kiss we'd shared many times there below the surface, but this time it came with such truth, I felt the shatter of any reservation I'd been forced to face before.

His hands left my cheeks, sliding and pressing into my back, over my wings, pulling me closer. The heat of his skin on mine was enough to burn me, flay me—sear me thoroughly until I could not separate Goddess from King.

"Ahem!"

He kissed my neck, driving a moan from my lips when his teeth grazed over the bite marks left there a year before.

"AH-HEM!"

I startled, holding onto Arthur's shoulders and turning my head to see Piffle, standing there covered in what only the deepest parts of the Veil could identify, and wringing his hands again.

"Apologies, Piff," Arthur started, pulling the strap of my gown back over my shoulder.

"Perhaps a bath is in order? It is one thing to be saved *again* on the brink of death, and entirely another to go at it in such... filth." He looked down at his own attire. "I suppose I could use a wash as well."

Arthur rose, pulling me up with him, slipping a hand underneath my knees and holding me at his chest. "After you, Piff," he said, nodding toward the northern corridor.

With a toothy grin, Piff led the way to fill our bath, and I wrapped my arms around the man I loved.

CHAPTER 50

Arthur

RESHINA WAS UNEQUIVOCALLY MINE, AND THE MOMENT Piff left to see to his own bath, I was kissing her hard against the marble inlaid along the walls of the washing room as steam rose in great billows scented with floral notes.

Just as feral, she had me stripped in seconds, blood flaked and crusted along our bodies, something far worse matted in our hair—we didn't care, we didn't have time to follow Piff's suggestion and bathe, we only had time to come together again.

My cock slid inside her pressed against the wall, and we quickly became undone. Where once I made love to my wife, now I made love to the woman who loved me back. I didn't know how her curse had been broken, how she'd saved me from death, her daughter from her illness, or what had happened in the western corridor, but I did know she loved me.

She repeated it over and over as I thrust into her, the sound of our bodies slapping together filling the warm air shifting around us. When she came, she came hard, crying out, biting down on my neck.

I saw stars, the moon, the edges of the Veil as I spilled into her wrapped tightly on my cock. She laughed as I plunged her into the bath, scrubbing her body inch by inch, taking my time with my favorite parts of her.

When we'd finally washed clean, I brought her to our bed, refusing to let her go. We lay on our sides, bodies pressed together and she told me of her journey to save her daughter. She explained how I'd broken her curse and how, with Piffle's help, she'd gotten me to Ishtak.

"You cannot tell me the rest," I concluded.

"No. But it will be revealed in time."

"You are free. You may leave whenever you'd like."

She shook her head. "No, Arthur. You are bound to the Underrealm and lands of Heartstone Castle for half of each year. And I am bound to you in that time as well."

I grunted. "And how is that curse broken?"

"I'm not telling."

I nipped her finger in my hand. "I'll get it out of you yet."

She laughed, a beautiful, carefree sound. "I'd rather keep that curse. I like it. It binds me to the man I love, and I will not be parted from him."

"I'll never get tired of it, you know. I'll never stop wanting to hear you say it."

Her lips brushed mine. "I love you, my husband. I do very much love you."

Epilogue

"IT IS UNFORTUNATE, MISTRESS," PIFFLE WHISPERED IN my ear, "that the Lady Seraphine was not here for last year's color."

I stole a glance in her direction. She sat next to Korven, draped in a deep pine green—the year's color of the Sprouting Festival. Both of them listened to my husband addressing his people at the podium in the center of Heartstone Wood. Seraphine held their baby, grinning broadly as Arthur spoke with more kindness and wisdom than any king his people had ever known.

Korven frowned, attempting to keep their wild little Avici in his lap.

"I agree with you, Piff. Though, Seraphine's beauty has no limitations."

He hummed, nodding. "Do you think she might accept a gown from me?"

I held back a laugh. "Have you already made it?"

"You know me well, Mistress," he giggled and I joined him, pressing my lips together tightly when Killian frowned my way.

"What are you whispering about?" Morella leaned in to ask, ignoring the elbow jab from her husband.

"Beautiful gowns," I said under my breath, bringing my attention back to Arthur.

"And so, it is with humility and great honor that I welcome you all to the first day of the Sprouting Festival, not as your king, but as a man ready to lead his people and deliver prosperity throughout all of Heartstone Wood."

Cheers erupted from the stands with almost everyone bolting from their seats, clapping and tossing petals into the air.

Seraphine nudged my son and he rose with reluctance, tossing his firstborn, Avici, up onto his shoulders and holding her legs in place—no doubt so he wouldn't need to partake in the applause.

Two months after the curse breaking, Arthur had finally been able to control the Beast well enough to return to the surface without the monster taking over—just in time for the start of the Sprouting Festival and the first family gathering of the royal Ravenfae.

As the crowd dispersed to begin the festivities, I met Arthur on the stage, kissing him soundly.

"Give me the truth, wife. How was my speech?"

"Kingly. Endearing." I pulled him close, whispering in his ear, "Will you wear the crown tonight when you fuck me, husband?"

His breathy laugh tickled my skin. "Tonight? Why the wait? I imagine there must be a—"

"King Arthur," Killian interrupted.

I moved aside to greet him, threading my fingers through Arthur's.

Killian held out his hand, king to king. "Good speech."

"Arthur!" Morella burst, squeezing in front of Killian and wrapping her arms around his neck. She kissed his cheek. "You were brilliant! Did you see the crowd? They were hanging on your every word!"

My husband laughed. "Thank you, Morella, for the praise

and for attending. Your mother has not paused a moment in planning your stay in Heartstone for weeks now."

Morella's face lit with joy. "Will you join us for the festivities, then? I hear it is tradition to play word games with the names of the flowers that grow here, is that true?" She didn't let him answer as he opened his mouth to speak. "I would love to try my hand at it! I think I'd do well!"

Killian grabbed her waist, her belly rounded with child. "You would crush any competition, Moh Dhóches."

They stared at each other in heated silence and my eyes darted back and forth between them with a brow raised.

Arthur kissed my cheek and hid a chuckle. "Well, yes, I'd be happy to join you just as soon as I borrow your mother for a few—"

"Arthur!" It was Seraphine's turn, shoving her way through the King and Queen of the Citrine Cliffs. She threw her arms around him and he caught her there, squeezing her tightly.

"Seraphine," he murmured. "It is wonderful to see you again. Long ago, I feared I never would get to see the beautiful woman I'd befriended so easily."

"And lied to," Korven muttered, following his wife.

Seraphine gripped Arthur's shoulders, shaking him slightly. "We must catch up. I want to know *everything*. Every single thing since that night in the tower. And you'd better not leave out the more gruesome details, nor the sordid ones." She glanced at me. "Is it true you pulled Reshina down underground by the ankle?"

"*Goddess damn me*," Korven sighed, transferring both of his children into Killian and Morella's arms. "Let me say my piece before I can leave you two to it."

He stood before Arthur, weighing him, his jaw flexing and his wings rustling behind him—something they'd always done of their own accord. With a deep inhale and release, he looked at me with a brow raised as if to say, *This, mother? This is who you love?*

I cocked my head, returning his look with a clear nod.

Finally, he held a hand out between them. "You broke my mother's curse."

Arthur took his hand, shaking it firmly. "I did."

"You love her?"

"I do."

Korven's mouth twisted. "I'm not calling you father."

A bellow of laughter, strong, deep, and beautiful lifted from my husband's chest. "Arthur's fine, Korven." He slapped his shoulder heartily. "Arthur will do."

SIX MONTHS WAS NOTHING. SIX MONTHS WAS THE BLINK of an eye when our days were spent in the quiet Underrealm reading and sharing books, sharing food and drink, sharing pleasure.

I was sure to imply the importance that Arthur allow the Beast to hunt on the surface for a few hours everyday, though I explained I could not give him the details of why. When our six months were over and we were released for another half year, we traveled to the Citrine Cliffs to meet the little princeling the king and queen had named Córmac, meaning son of the raven. Chubby and adored by his parents, we spent our month visiting, stealing him away as often as we could. Arthur and I cooed over our grandchildren, soaking in our time with three little royal Ravenfae.

We spent the rest of the months away from the Underrealm in the Brackish Wood. There, I addressed the concerns of my people, spending time healing them in their homes, and meeting the next generation of our faekind.

Arthur eased into his role as the husband of a Goddess beautifully—introducing himself, and listening to the stories kept hidden within the Brackish Wood. Within the blink of an eye, our six months were over and we made our way back to the Underrealm. Piffle returned as well, having traveled all over Revelry, collecting trinkets and fabrics alike.

A month in from our return, Arthur woke me with a kiss. "Something has arrived and I do not possess the patience for you to wake on your own to see it."

"It had better be your tongue on my skin or your cock in my hand, King of Heartstone," I groaned, turning away from him, seeking cool sheets.

His laugh tickled my neck. "Better than that."

"No such thing," I murmured into my pillow.

"Alright, an additional gift I'll give to you this morning."

I finally turned towards him. "What could be worth waking me early, then?"

He held a book bound in emerald green cloth. "I received this from Piffle last night and have spent all morning adding notes in the margins."

I sat up, taking the book into my hands. The corners were reinforced with gold filigree brackets and the end pages detailed black thorns across a sketch of my crown. I flipped to the title page. "*The Goddess and the Beast*." I traced the letters of the raised ink, too filled with emotion to speak.

"I had the story we penned bound in Riche by the finest artisans. Everything's there. Down to each salacious detail. I've already begun my notes and left you plenty of room to—"

"I adore you, husband." I cupped his cheek with the flood of tears brimming in my eyes. "I love you, and have loved you, and I swear on the Veil I will love you."

He took my hand, bringing my palm to his lips. "Turn to chapter thirty-eight."

I did and there in the margins he'd written, "Care for a repeat?"

I skimmed the chapter detailing the night I'd poisoned him with my last attempt to escape the curse and the body worshiping he'd done after.

I snapped the book shut, my blood heating, desire tugging at my lower belly. "You read my mind."

His hands gripped my hips, pulling me on top of his lap. "I know it well." He gripped the back of my head, kissing me hard, loving me wildly, like a feral Beast from beyond the Veil.

Also by

CHELSEY ANN TOMPKINS

READY FOR MORE FROM *A REALM OF REVELRY*?

CURSE & SPINDLE, A SLEEPING BEAUTY RETELLING

When a human woman is thrust into her role as princess, she is betrothed to a prince she loathes. But as she's walking down the aisle, the Ravenfae Prince of her childhood swoops in to deliver the curse meant for her at birth. The curse has grown powerful over her 25 years, and now, with the devastatingly handsome Ravenfae Prince's help, she will search to find someone to kiss her lips and save them both from the worst fate...if they don't give into their own desires first.

Straw & Gold, A Rumplestiltskin Retelling

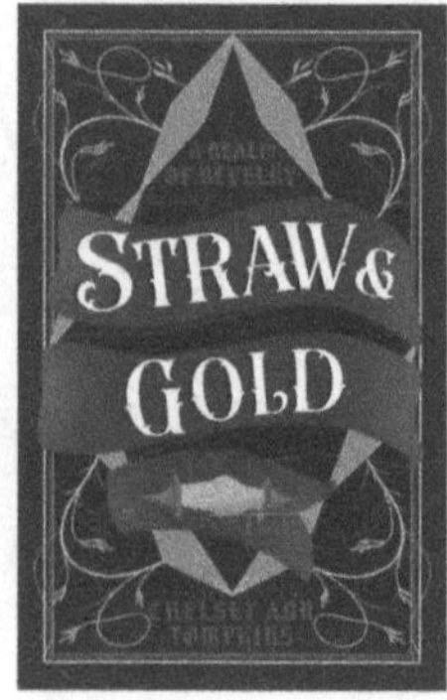

When a Ravenfae princess is bound by contract to marry a distant king, she plays along to save her brother's wife from a mortal death. Bound to her husband by marriage and a fae bargain, she must discover the name he can never speak to change her sister-in-law's fate and save the king she has come to love before he is taken from her forever.

Looking forward to the next faerietale retelling? Follow CHELSEY ANN TOMPKINS to keep up to date with the next release in A Realm of Revelry Series!

More from Chelsey Ann Tompkins

A Conduit of Light Trilogy

Read this complete adult fantasy romance trilogy where love knows no bounds, and for one ancient force, time has no meaning. Available on Kindle Unlimited and major booksellers.

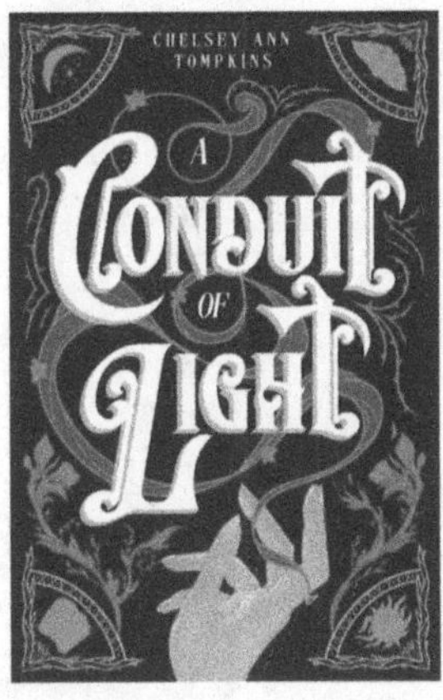

If you enjoyed this book, (or any book!) I'd like to encourage you to rate/review it. Algorithms from sites like Amazon, Goodreads, and Barnes & Noble base their recommendations of books from a book's number of reviews and ratings. These reviews and ratings are especially important to indie authors like me who do not have high budgets or marketing resources to gain a large readership. We depend on people like you to help us, so thank you for your support. Happy reading!

Acknowledgments

Reshina's story came to me over the course of writing the lives of her children. I knew when starting *A Realm of Revelry* that I wanted to get to her book and to tell the story of an ancient goddess. When it came time to write it down, it was far more difficult than I imagined. But inspiration comes from the most obvious of places: the women I admire in my life.

If Rachel was a six-hundred-year-old Goddess, I would not be surprised in the slightest. When this woman has two feet on the ground, she is unstoppable. Rach, I have loved you all six-hundred of your years, I'm sure of it. Thank you for adoring Revelry.

Des, you have encouraged my writing more than you could know. I adore that we share the same love of so many things from whimsical sticky-notes to epic and all-consuming fantasy series. Thank goodness for books and double margaritas.

To my PA Jordan, I am beyond proud of myself for snagging you into this whole thing. Not only are you hilarious, you are so well-versed in this community, and I cannot imagine taking along with me a better cheerleader and badass who gets done what needs to get done. I cannot wait to see you continue to thrive in your roles.

To the Library Cats and the Catnapped Collective, thank you for all the excitement on every post and mention of anything I'm working on or have been working on. You push me forward, and I'm so happy to keep writing all the goodness you love to read.

It takes a lot of time to write a book, even a short one, and I must thank my husband for the sixth time for taking on all the extra work that comes with being married to a woman with big dreams.

Finally, thank you to my children who are so very curious about what their mother is writing, are never given details, and continue to be excited about my books anyway. I love you two forever and ever.

Thank you, readers! Cheers to the next tale in A Realm of Revelry!

About the Author

Chelsey Ann Tompkins was born to be a storyteller, specializing in tales of magic and swoon-worthy romance. Her adolescence was spent reading countless historical romance novels and classic literature, leading to a love of brooding men and strong-willed female characters. When she is not dreaming up heartbreaking romance stories, you can find her brewing yet another vanilla latte, at the library with her kids, or reading while indulging in the blissful silence a bubble bath provides. She resides near Seattle with her husband and two children.

@chelseyanntompkins